a banana split for christmas and other stories

The Matchmaker Baker Series
Book One

ames b. winterbourne

Illustrated by
reina diaz

Artwork by Reina Diaz

Cover Design by Booked Forever Shop

❀ Created with Vellum

For all the girls who can't call a males anatomy either a cock or dick. This is for girls who call dicks popsicles. You did this to me, and now I will never look at ice cream the same again...

This book may contain nuts. Please be advised that I do not condone anyone doing anything like what the people in this book do to food in real life. This is a fantasy story... Well, it's someone's fantasy.

Content Warnings and Kinks: sexual content with nonhuman anatomy, food play, somnophilia, dub-con, fat shaming, and body image issues.

Just to be clear, the main FMC loves her body and thinks anyone who has a problem with it can suck a fuck, but that doesn't mean that words don't hurt, and sometimes they do hurt, and that makes people question everything.

playlist

1. All I Want For Christmas Is You by Mariah Carey
2. Ice Cream - New Young Pony Club
3. FU In My Head - Cloudy June
4. Cruel Summer - Taylor Swift
5. S&M - Rihanna
6. Ice Cream - Blackpink with Selena Gomez
7. Santa Claus Is Coming to Town - Mariah Carey

one

· · ·

*T*here was a point in time when I had everything. A loving, caring boyfriend, a mother that didn't treat me like shit because I was happily going to get engaged, and a job that I liked enough because I got to see my boyfriend every day. He'd send me flowers, chocolate, and especially ice cream, my favorite. And then everything came crashing down.

"Duncan dumped you a month ago, Katie. It's time you forget that fucker," my friend Libby says. "It's almost Christmas time, and I don't want you to be a statistic."

"Libs, not cool." Jason nudges her.

"Okay, stop it, guys. That's enough." I huff.

I look over the top of my computer at Libby and Jason, my two best friends. They look like they're on a mission for something, but I have no idea what.

"I don't want to date anyone. Plus, fuck Christmas.

1

I want to focus on work."

"You're a mean one, Miss Grinch. Also, you hate your job." Jason says.

Merial, who works at the desk beside me, gasps, and Jason rolls his eyes. "Right, I'm sure you just *love* your job as Duncan's secretary, Merial. A real dream come true."

Merial ducks her head, and I look back at my computer and sigh. I've been working on this cost sheet for hours, even though I don't need to. But whenever Duncan walks by, I want to look like I'm doing something productive so I don't have to look at his regretful, muddy brown eyes. I know he feels sorry that he broke up with me, but I also know that we're never getting back together. Ever. He broke up with me on Halloween, ruining all our holiday plans. My family's Thanksgiving last week was full of pitying looks. And now Christmas is coming up, and I decided I'm not dealing with that shit again. So, I told my family I had tons of work and no time to go home for the holidays. Thinking of just spending the holidays alone sounds like the perfect way to ignore the pain in my chest.

It's mostly his mother nagging him and telling him that he lost the best thing he ever had that makes him like this. I would know because the crazy woman has been calling me nonstop, trying to do anything to get me to take her son back. Of course, telling me it's not a big deal to drop a few pounds to get my boyfriend back isn't helping her cause.

Duncan dumped me because I gained twenty

pounds in the last two years, but it's partially his fault. He loved sending me sweets and filling me with ice cream every chance. He had a thing for buying me food and spoiling me that way, but when I gained weight, it was apparently a big no-no.

I love my body. I love that I went from practically starving myself before I met him, always eating celery and only drinking water, to finding my love for sweets again. But lately, whenever I look at an ice cream sundae, I wonder if it's worth it. I'm a single secretary at a dead-end job I hate, living by myself. I don't even have a cat! My apartment is just big enough for a small tree in the corner and some decorations that make it look nicer than it usually does. It's not a bad apartment. It's just small with thin walls. I can hear my neighbors on the other side going at it and making me feel uncomfortable and lonely, especially since Duncan dumped me. I've banged on the wall countless times, but that never stops them. Duncan and I never made them bang on the wall when we had sex, so that says something.

"Let's go to lunch," Libby suggests. "And I know the perfect place that Danielle told me about."

"Danielle has expensive taste." I frown knowing that my bank account won't approve of my big spending. With holiday gifts, I was forced to buy family and friends, student loans, plus planning my sister's bachelorette party and paying for everything; I'm not looking to spend my remaining money on a fancy lunch.

"The holidays are coming up. It's an early Christmas present." Jason places a hand on mine.

I look at them and their puppy dog eyes. Jason has beautiful blue eyes that contrast with his dark skin, while Libby has chocolate brown eyes that are so expressive if she wants to look sad and pitiful, you want to give her anything she asks for to make her happy again.

"Okay. But I'm not ordering a salad." I get up from my desk and grab my purse. My friends both smile at each other.

"Oh, believe me when I say there's no salad where we're going," Libby says, and I catch her winking at Jason who smirks.

And there isn't.

We pull up to a small bakery resembling a cottage in the middle of Los Angeles. It has a sign that says The Matchmaker Baker.

I furrow my brow. "A bakery? I thought we were getting lunch."

"They have sandwiches..." Libby parks the car. "But also specialties."

"What's specialties?"

"You'll see," Jason practically jumps in his seat. He's so giddy it gets me a little excited, too. "And they have a sale for the holidays!"

"I do love a good sale," I say. "But I'm not getting anything Christmas-themed."

They both look at each other and say, "Bah-humbug."

We make our way into the quaint bakery. The floor is checkered, and the counter with a display of the most decadent baked goods is in the middle of the room. There is more than one display of yummy baked things, too. The room is covered in Christmas lights, with green and red cupcakes, candy, and sweets.

Christmas used to be my favorite holiday. Duncan would make a fabulous Christmas dinner, and we'd spend the day just in each other's presence. I'd bake my heart out, and he'd eat everything. He always said if I wasn't such a good secretary, I should quit my job and become a baker. The week before, we'd decorate the Christmas tree at his small house in Los Feliz before returning to my place in Tarzana and decorating.

I try not to think about him as I look at the bakery walls covered in candies in the shape of men and women. Some are huge candy canes. Others are just regular chocolate or chocolate that's holiday-themed. There's dark chocolate, milk chocolate, white chocolate, chocolate with nuts, sprinkles, and fruits. Then, in the display case are baked goods, skillfully designed figures made of various cake flavors, and cookies shaped like ripped men. I look at my friends and blush at the menu on the wall. There's a list of qualities you want in a partner and the type of ice cream that correlates with it. I gape at it.

"This is... Uh."

"Deliciously sexual?" Jason looks at the case with his nose pressed up to it. "That one. That one's mine." He points to an obscenely muscled chocolate gingerbread cookie with icing that outlines every ripple of the male's muscles.

I glance at the case and am in awe at what I see. Every sweet is in a different shape or size, with different faces. None look alike.

"This is insane! This is pure art!" I'm in awe. As an amateur baker, I can't imagine the detail and work that goes into these. It makes me feel so inadequate with my own baked goods that Duncan and my friends always compliment me for. I wanted to attend culinary school at one point, but my parents weren't for it. They said I needed a real job and shouldn't waste my time. So, I studied business management, and now I'm the office manager and lead secretary at a huge law firm. Well, I was until recently.

"Why, thank you," A large woman walks out of the back, drying her hands on her apron. "I'm Mrs. Owens, the shop owner. It's a pleasure to meet you all."

She's absolutely gorgeous with her blonde curled hair, beauty mark above her lip, and vibrant blue eyes. She's like a plus-size Marilyn Monroe but with a few age lines.

"You make all of this?"

She nods with a smile, dimples popping out on her cheeks. "I do."

"This is incredible!" Libby gazes at the candy men. She points to a milk chocolate peppermint bar shaped like a beautiful man. His head is shaved, his big muscles are detailed, and chunks of candy canes are all over him. "That one. That's the one I want."

Mrs. Owens smiles. "Good choice. I call him

Pepper. He's a milk chocolate peppermint bar, after all."

She goes up to the candy man and takes him off the shelf. Then she places him by the register.

I'm still taking in the whole shop while both my friends check out.

"What can I get for you, sweetie?" Mrs. Owens asks me.

I look at the menu and say, "Do you make your ice cream?"

"Yes, with whole milk and the freshest ingredients. What do you like?"

"I don't want anything that's holiday-themed. I'm not in the mood for Christmas this year."

"Oh, that's so sad. I love the holidays. But I understand. I can think of a few things that we have that you'd like."

"She loves banana splits," Libby says.

"Oh my god, does the banana split have a banana as a dick?" Jason asks.

I can feel my neck heat from his words. I'm no prude, but jeez!

"He does, and his balls are chocolate truffles with sea salt. His fingers are made of mini-ice cream cones, too."

"Oh my god," I place my hands on my heated cheeks.

"He has gum drops for eyes. He's vanilla flavored, with a cherry nose, red sprinkles for lips, and white square sprinkles for teeth. Gorgeous if you ask me."

"Can I... Um... Take it to go?"

"Everything is to go, dear. Well, except for what's on the lunch menu," she points to a tiny little menu at the end of the list of male and female ice cream flavors. "None of our sandwiches are in the shapes of men and women. Don't worry. I don't promote that kind of behavior *in* my store." She winks at me, and I have no idea what she thinks I will do with the ice cream.

"Here, let me get you your ice cream to go. But it's always better the next day."

"The next day? It's ice cream." I laugh.

She shrugs. "I'm told people enjoy it the day after the most. They don't want to dig in right away when they can post tons of pictures on social media," she chuckles.

She goes into the back of the store, and I give my friends a confused look.

"It says that on the sign out front," Jason frowns. "You should wait 24 hours before you eat anything in the store because everything tastes better the next day."

"Whatever," Libby licks her lips as she looks at her candy man. "I'm going to take so many pictures with this guy," she points to her chocolate. "And then tomorrow morning, when I wake up, I will eat him up."

"I don't know if I can wait that long," Jason looks like he's practically drooling. "I love cookies."

"Oh, please do wait!" Mrs. Owens returns to the room with a plastic to-go box she hands me. I look down at my colossal banana-split man, and my eyes widen. I've never been attracted to food before (other than wanting to devour it), but this guy looks like my dream man. He has medium-length dried hot fudge hair and blue gum drops for his eyes. He has everything she said he would. I don't know how she does it, but she has a chocolate mold over the body of the ice cream that is just as detailed as the gingerbread man that Jason bought.

"Now, take the white chocolate mold off when you get home, and you can eat that tonight, but wait until tomorrow to eat the ice cream. It needs to freeze better. I promise you'll enjoy it like you've never enjoyed sweets before." Mrs. Owens smiles kindly.

I nod, still entranced by the hot ice cream I'm looking at. "Uh, okay."

She smiles, and as I take out my credit card, Libby hands Mrs. Owens her card and says, "It's her Christmas present. It's on us."

"Oh! A Christmas present? How lovely!" Mrs. Owens claps her hands, "This is on the house!"

We all gape at her but don't argue as she waves us goodbye. "Enjoy your sweets, kids!"

We leave in shock.

"I can't wait to eat this man up," Jason licks his lips.

"You have to wait," Libby bats his arm.

Jason huffs looks at his cookie, and frowns.

I look at my ice cream and don't feel like eating him anymore. This is serious art, and I don't know how long this ice cream will last, but I'm keeping it in my freezer well past the holidays.

two

. . .

*L*ibby and Jason call us all out sick for the rest of the day, and we return to my apartment, where I immediately place my Mr. Ice Cream in the freezer.

We order pizza and beer, and they insist on watching Christmas romance movies, which almost makes me gag. I used to love these; hell, I would watch them all year round, but now they make my chest ache and my stomach whirl just thinking about love during the holidays.

Libby is about to pass out when Jason says, "We better go. It's getting late, and I have court tomorrow."

"And I have... stuff for my sister to do." I lie, looking around my apartment and debating whether to remove all the decorations my sister put up. She decorated a silver fake Christmas tree with our ornaments that I bought with Duncan and some childhood ones that my sister, Krissy, and I made together. My sister snuck them away from my parents' home, trying to cheer me up to remember the fun and happy Christmas we had as children and every year, even before Duncan came into my life. They do nothing for me except remind me of how lonely I was before Duncan and how lonely I am now. Fuck, I am a statistic. Depression during the holidays sucks ass.

"Right," he nods, frowning. "Your sister's wedding is on New Year's Eve."

"I need some time to decompress before I go home and deal with my mom, that's for sure."

Jason frowns but nods and he and Libby hug me goodbye as they exit my apartment with their sweets from *Matchmaker* Baker.

I plop on my couch and am about to turn on a horror movie because fuck Christmas and romance, but my phone rings.

I pick it up and see my mother's face flash across the screen. It's eight pm, and she hasn't called me all day. She's been too busy planning my little sister's wedding to contact me as usual every morning and night.

I answer the phone and say, "Hey mom."

"Hi, sweetie-pie!" She says happily.

"What's up?"

"I just wanted to check on you. Sorry for calling so late. Your sister had a little tantrum with her fiancé today. I've been doing damage control all day!"

"Is Krissy okay?" I love my baby sister, and I've always hated her fiancé, whom she met a year ago and

11

who proposed almost immediately. He always seemed like a douchebag to me, with his blonde slicked-back hair, polo shirt, and pants that were always high above his ankles. His name is Chad, too, which doesn't help. Then again, I dated a guy named Duncan.

"Yes, yes. I was wondering if you and Duncan have made up yet."

I sigh. "Mom, Duncan dumped me. We're not getting back together. He's not interested in me anymore."

"Well, can't you just lose a few pounds? A smaller bridesmaid dress might be cheaper, too. Plus, I hate that you're missing Christmas because you picked up so much work to distract yourself."

I cringe. "I already have my dress, Mom, and I really don't need you to fat shame me like that shithead."

"I'm not trying to fat shame you," she sighs. We've had this conversation over and over again. It's getting super old. The only people who don't give me a hard time about my weight are my friends, Dad, and Krissy. "I was just saying—"

"Leave her alone, Melody," Dad calls out in the background.

I smile at his defense. "The guy is a little shit. His name is Duncan, for Christ's sake. Who names their kids that? His parents must have looked into his eyes when he was born and thought, 'Ah, you look like you're going to have all the personality of a rice cake. We shall name you Duncan!'" I try not to laugh.

"I talked to his mother. He's felt guilty since the breakup and told her he misses you like crazy. He was wrong to do that. His friends were making fun of him—"

"I don't care that his friends were making fun of him. He's an asshole!" I snap. "And I don't need this from you."

She's quiet on the phone for a moment before I hear the inevitable dramatic sniff. "I'm sorry, sweetheart." Her fake crying makes me roll my eyes. This woman taught me how to cry on command when she wanted me to audition for a commercial as a child. I didn't get the role because no one wants you to cry when trying to sell Target clothes. The makeup ran down my face and stained the clothing they put me in, and Mom had to buy them from the crew. I was a failure then and a failure now, too.

"I know, Mom. I need to sleep, okay? It's late, and it's been a long day. I'll talk to you tomorrow, okay?"

"Of course, sweetie." She sounds all cheery again. "Just think about it. Maybe going on a diet won't be so bad. And then you both can come to Christmas!"

"Goodbye, Mother." I snap and hang up the phone.

I frown and feel the need to eat something sweet to get the taste of the bad conversation with my mom out of my mouth.

I go over to my refrigerator and open the freezer. I look at the hot ice cream man and open his packaging before taking out the white chocolate mold over his body. When I do, I see that the mold did an excellent job preserving the ice cream into the shape of a hot guy. I close the freezer and eat the chocolate. It tastes sweet and light and makes me even more hungry. I look back at my phone and then at my ice cream and chocolate-covered fingers. I could lick my fingers clean and savor the taste of the ice cream, or I could wash my hands, go to bed, and then think about starting an exercise routine in the morning.

I nibble on my lip before I sigh and go to wash my hands.

I get ready for bed, brushing my teeth, washing my face, and getting into my satin sleep shorts and top. It's soft and feels good on my skin. I look at myself in the mirror, and I don't see the fat girl everyone makes me out to be. I see a curvy woman with thick thighs, a nice ass, and big breasts. I have a tummy, but my boobs are bigger than it, so I don't think that I look terrible. I just look like I have huge boobs. I throw my hair into a bun and get into bed. My silk sheets feel cool on my skin. It's hot out, even in December. That's what I get for living in California.

I turn off my light and fall into a deep sleep.

*K*isses rain across my cheeks. It's a cool wet touch; I revel in it since we've had such hot weather. Then hard, solid lips press against my own. They taste sugary sweet, and as teeth sink into my bottom lip, I moan. He tastes like chocolate fudge, and his tongue laps at my bottom lip, making me open to him. His tongue is rough, different than I've ever touched before. He tastes like whipped cream and cherries as he tangles his tongue with mine. My eyes are shut as I give in to him. His ice-cold palms and ribbed fingers mold my breast. I arch into his touch, and he uses his sticky fingers to tweak my nipple. I gasp and cry out, nearly coming from the feeling of being touched, which I haven't been in a long time.

His mouth roams down from my lips to my breast, and he nips at my nipple, his teeth sharp but soft at the same time. I groan as his damp hand tease down my body, creating a mess as his fingers reach my clit. I complain as my wetness mixes with his. The roughness of his fingers makes me tease as he twirls them around my clit.

It feels so good, better than I ever thought it could be. I mean, I'm dreaming of fucking a man made of ice cream. He's still sucking on my breast, pouring his creamy thickness over my body.

Then his fingers trail from my clit to my hole, and before I know it, he thrusts his ice cream cone fingers into my pussy. It doesn't feel anything but smooth with ridges. Their tips aren't sharp but round, and I gasp at the feeling of thickness and yet softness of his touch. He thrusts his fingers in and out of me, and I cry out as the thickness from the curves hits me right where I need him. I come crying out and quaking around him.

"That's right, baby. Just like that," his voice is deep

and husky, very different from what I'd expect from a sweet ice cream man.

He removes his finger, and then, before I know it, I peek my dreamy eye open and see him, sweating cream over me. He's dripping his milkiness over my body as he kneels before me, stroking his very monstrous banana cock. His balls are salty chocolate truffles, and I really want to lick them.

"You ready for me?"

"Yes," I breathe, and then he leans down and says against my lips, my nostrils flaring at the sweet scent of sugar.

"I scream," he inches slowly into me. I gasp at his girth. "You scream," he stretches me further. "We all scream for..."

Then he thrusts his engorged cock into me, and I scream. It's so thick and hard. He's definitely not ripe yet. He pounds into me, pulling my leg up over his frozen shoulder, and slams his soft, sticky pelvis against me.

"Fuck you feel so good. So... real." He moans. "You taste so good."

He grunts as he pulls out of me abruptly, and I practically sob from the loss of him. Then he flips me over, and I make an oomph sound before he thrusts right back into me, slapping his coned fingers against my ass hard.

I can imagine a crisscrossed indent into my skin. His chocolate balls slap against my clit, and they're hard but smooth. I can't think. I can't breathe. Then he thrusts faster into me, and I come so hard.

He groans out a "Fuck," and pulls out before he comes all over my back. It's hot, and I smell chocolate. Is his cum hot fudge?

He collapses on top of my back, and I'm soaked as he melts over me. I'm a mix of emotions. Sexually, I'm sated, but I'm also starving.

My body aches most deliciously.

He uses his tongue to lick up the mix of sweat and cream on my back.

"My, my. You're even sweeter than I am." He growls against me.

Then I fall back asleep. Even though I'm already asleep. At least, I think.

three

. . .

I bat my eyes open as I take in the sun peeking through my blinds. My body feels tense and achy, like I've been fucked within an inch of my life. I think back on my smutty dream with ice cream, of all things. I nibble on my lip, feeling embarrassed and thankful that no one will ever know.

"I dreamt about fucking ice cream. I don't know if that means I need to go to church or on a diet. Or therapy. Probably therapy," I sigh as I sit up from bed. I'm not sticky like I dreamed of being, but in my dreams, I also took a hot shower, being placed there by a godlike ice cream man, and then changed into another set of pajamas, a cotton pair with ice cream cones all over it.

I laugh at the craziness of it all. I can't help but look down at my PJs and gasp. It's the set of jammies I put on after the dream shower. I touch my hair, and it's still slightly damp.

I jump up and run into my kitchen, where I begin

to hyperventilate. It was a dream. That's all it was. I did take a shower before I went to bed, and I could have just been tired enough not to notice that I put on the wrong sleepwear.

I slowly step toward my refrigerator and close my eyes. "It was just a dream. Just a dream."

I open my freezer, my mouth drops open, and my heart races as I find that my ice cream boyfriend isn't there.

"What the fuck!"

"You know," the husky voice from my dream says as the fully corporeal ice cream man that fucked me last night, *not* in my dreams, stands there with a spoon full of frozen yogurt that he stuffs in his mouth. He licks his sprinkle lips before saying, "I don't understand why people eat this shit. Ice cream is so much better."

My eyes bulge, and I think I might faint. I don't. I'm seriously looking at a talking ice cream shaped like a man. "Did you... Did we?"

"Did we fuck last night? Yes. You fell asleep right after. Talk about a sugar crash."

"I think I need to sit down," I say as I go to my couch and take a seat. "I... You..."

He smiles and takes a seat on my desk chair. My apartment is small, and my living room also is used as an office and dining area. The Christmas decorations make it look even tinier. My sister decorated my desk with tinsel and Christmas figurines. It's super cramped in here. It looks even smaller with this tall, muscular ice cream man in it.

"You're going to get my chair all dirty."

"And sticky." He smirks. "But I've realized that once I move from place to place, my ice cream melts away like magic."

"Like magic," I mutter. "Yeah, that's a word for it. I've gone insane. I'm having a nervous breakdown. That's what this must be. I'm so lonely and depressed that I've gone crazy. I'm dealing with the holiday blues. I've imagined I've fucked a man made of ice cream, for fucks sake! And he's a cannibal!"

"I'm not a cannibal. This," he points to the yogurt container in his hand with his spoon. "Is almond fro-yo. It was very far back of your freezer." I don't know how he's not melting and that he looks like an ice sculpture made of ice cream. But when he claps his hand, I notice the creaminess of his thigh jiggle, and he pulls his cone fingers away and frowns. "If only the cream disappeared when I touched myself. Anyway, I'm guessing the fro-yo isn't yours. Is there someone I should be worried about?"

"There's no competition," I laugh sadly. I'm so pitiful that I'm talking to my imaginary ice cream man. "And there never will be. I'll be put in a mental institute."

"You're being dramatic, and I'm all real, baby. I'm the realist thing in your life."

I shake my head. "Please stop talking. You're making it worse."

"Tell me, Katie," he gets up from his seat. At first, I notice white cream all over the chair before it vanishes into thin air. He walks over to my couch and sits next to me. He places the frozen yogurt on the coffee table with the spoon stuffed inside of it. "Is your body sore?"

I turn and gape at him.

"Do you think that happened just by having a dream and fucking yourself with your fingers? Because it wasn't you that made you come so hard last night that you passed out and were in such a daze that I had to help shower you. I almost melted. But my ice cream regenerated when I went back into the freezer."

"Went back into the freezer?"

"After I put you to bed, I went back into the freezer to sleep. You wore me out. I mean, fuck. I've never come so hard in my life. The amount of hot fudge that came out of me." He shakes his head. Ice cream drips onto my couch, and I cringe at how I'll need to clean this up. "I'm shocked you're not pregnant with my little popsicle."

I jump up from my seat. "I can't get pregnant from a fucking ice cream sundae!"

"Banana split." He clarifies.

"Whatever! That's not possible. Oh my god. I'm going to get the worst UTI." I cringe, thinking about how to explain this to my gynecologist.

"Maybe, but tell me it wasn't worth it? When was the last time you had such amazing sex?"

"I wouldn't call having sex with ice cream amazing. I love a good sweet, but this is so wrong. So wrong... I'll never be allowed in an ice cream parlor again. They'll all get restraining orders against me. I'll always have to be five hundred feet away from an ice cream shop. And what if there's an ice cream man driving by?"

"You may think this is wrong, but it's so right." He says, touching mine and pulling me onto his ice-cold lap. The ice cream seeps through my pajama bottoms, and I shiver at the wet touch.

"Let's just start over, okay?" He asks.

"I don't know how to start over with a banana split."

"I'm your ice cream boyfriend. That's what they call us at the store. We're supposed to fulfill your every desire. Boy, I'm glad you picked me over all the other guys. People have been buying up Christmas-themed goodies all week."

"There are others! Do they all fuck humans? Is this all ice cream?"

"Only from that shop. The owner is a witch."

"A witch!"

"She is a matchmaker of sorts and just wants people to have all their desires fulfilled. There's hunger in everyone, sexually and food-wise. And she wants to cater to all. I'll make you happy, I swear. I promise." He smiles sweetly at me, and my heart skips a beat.

I shake myself out of my daze and jump up from his lap. Suddenly, my body dries from his ice cream. I'm not sticky either, like I expect. "Huh."

"See, I told you. It's all part of the magic. Though after we had sex, there were some remnants of cream and fudge on you."

I sit back down on the couch and look at my banana-split boyfriend. *He's not your boyfriend!*

"What exactly is the purpose of all this? It's not like I can take you home for the holidays." I don't know why I'm worried about that. "It's sad if you think about it. She's setting up lonely people with food?"

"Food is comfort, and don't you want a comfortable relationship with your significant other too? It's the best of both worlds."

"But I..."

"Anyway, I got you something." He stuffs his hand into his ice cream stomach. I scream at the sight of the fingers slamming into his ripped abdomen. My eyes roam down to see if his banana is on display, but it's not. It's covered by ice cream.

His body is like a sculpture of a beautiful, hot man. He has a fucking eight-pack and muscles everywhere, though they're dripping with vanilla cream.

He pulls a full banana split in a bowl from his stomach and says, "I know you have been having a tough time, and I thought maybe this might make you feel a little better. You were thinking of dieting last night, but I don't want you to lose a pound."

I force a fake laugh and take the ice-cold bowl that isn't even from my kitchen into my hands.

"Eat it," he says as he pulls a spoon from his stomach.

"I..." I look at the banana split that seems so tempting and then at him. "I think I'm good."

"Seriously? I'm not offended that you eat a banana

split in front of me. My goal is to make you happy and to do that, I'm supposed to sate you in all ways."

"This is like... not cannibalism, really, but you look almost human-ish, and I'm eating what you're made of."

"I know, weird, but you'll enjoy it. Believe me." He smiles sweetly, and I swear his round face, like a scope of ice cream, has dimples.

I take the spoon from his hand and glance at the delicious banana split. There are peanuts, cherries, a split banana, hot fudge, and vanilla ice cream. I gulp, feeling almost sick, but at the same time, I *am* hungry.

Slowly, with shaky hands, I dig the spoon into the ice cream, and as I bring it to my lips, the ice cream boyfriend melts down the couch, and I scream.

"Keep eating," his melted self says. I bring the spoon to my lips, even though I don't know how my hands are steady, and take a bite. Just as I do, my shorts are pulled from my body, and suddenly, an ice-cold wet tongue flicks across my clit. I moan, and my eyes shudder closed. I don't know if it's from the sweet goodness in my mouth or what he's starting to do to my body. His dripping hands grab hold of my thighs as he positions me in a way where he can devour my pussy like I've never had anyone done before.

"Take another bite," he growls against my most intimate parts.

"I... I don't think I can." My body shivers from the cold and lust.

"Believe me when I say I can feel you when you eat

that ice cream. So you lick that spoon clean, and I'll lick you clean."

I moan as he twirls his sweet tongue around my clit, making me wetter than I've ever been. It's not just an average tongue, either. I look down and see that it's shaped like a popsicle... A cherry popsicle. My eyes bulge for a second before the firm texture of his dripping tongue mixed with his cream brings me close to coming.

I don't know if the wetness is from myself or his touch, but he keeps at it, and suddenly, his tight cones make me feel so full I gasp, and my body jolts up. He uses his other hand to hold my body still. "My cream will make it easy. It won't hurt. You won't be dry. I'll fuck your ass with my creamy thick fingers too."

I moan as he slowly enters my asshole with his edible fingers and continues eating my pussy.

I cry out as he thrusts them in and out and then moves his tongue down to my entrance, making me groan at the loss of his tongue on my clit. Then his popsicle tongue grows longer and thicker, and it feels weird but so good, too. He thrusts it into me, and I cry out. I convulse around him, and he moans, pushing his fingers in and out of my ass faster.

I quake around him. It feels dirty, sticky, and oh-so-sweet. And suddenly, the feeling is so overwhelming I scream without being able to control myself, and liquid squirts from me and into his face. He pulls his tongue free of my pussy and removes his fingers. Then he laps up my juices, mixing my cum with his milky cream.

He looks up at me with his blue gumdrop eyes and growls, "You are so fucking delicious."

"That means a lot coming from a dessert." My voice is slurred from the pleasure.

His sprinkled lips morph into a beaming smile. "You practically strangled my popsicle."

"How did the strawberry become so... Long?"

He smirks and sticks out his tongue to show that it's not just the frozen popsicle but the stick too.

"Oh fucking hell," I slap my hand across my face. "I just came around a popsicle stick."

"You did. And it was fucking fantastic."

My phone buzzes from somewhere in the room, and I get to my feet. My legs are wobbly as I stumble over to my desk, where I pick up my phone and see a text from my ex, Duncan.

DUNCAN

I'm so sorry, Honeybear. I miss you so much. Please, please talk to me. I can't bear the silence anymore.

My heart hurts at the sight of it, and I glance back at my ice cream boyfriend, who's now shoving the bowl of banana split back into his gut.

I check my phone and notice the time.

"I'm going to be late for work!"

"Oh?"

"Is there... Is there something I can call you besides my ice cream boyfriend or a banana split man? Ben? Jerry?"

He frowns and I think he's thinking about it. He doesn't have eyebrows, so it's hard to tell.

"Oh! How about Rocky? Like Rocky Road Ice Cream."

"This is getting out of hand," I mumble as I head to my bedroom. My body isn't sticky or wet from anything he's done to me like it was moments ago after he made me come, but I head to the shower anyway.

"I'd offer company," Rocky says from the doorway as I hop in the shower and hurry. "But I'd melt, and I don't know if I'd come back to life from that."

I don't respond as I wash my hair and my body. Everything is sore, but tingles at the same time. It's like a real man just took my body the way he wanted it. But it was so different, too. Sex with Rocky is the best I've ever had. I cringe at that realization.

I finish in the shower and get out, only to find him gone. I cover myself with a towel and look around my bedroom to see if he's there. "Rocky?"

There's no answer. I dress and exit my bathroom before glancing around my apartment for him. He's nowhere in sight. I go over to the freezer and close my eyes. "Was it all a dream?"

I open the freezer and there he is. He's frozen solid in the same position I bought him, minus the white chocolate cover. A part of me is relieved that maybe this was all a dream, but another part feels weirded out and uncomfortable that I've had dreams about an ice cream man, literal ice cream man, fucking me. It was all a dream, though.

I'm about to close the freezer when I notice the banana split bowl next to him in the freezer.

I gasp and slam the door. I'm shaking as I head out of my apartment. I see my neighbor Jenna locking her door, and when she sees me, she smirks at me. "About time you got some good lovin', girl. Though maybe try not to do it at two in the morning." She pats my shoulder before walking away.

I shut my eyes as I lean my head against my front door. "This can't be happening. This can't be happening."

"Oh," a voice echoes from inside my apartment. "It is baby."

I shriek before I rush out of the building and pretend like this never happened.

four

. . .

J get to work and go straight to my desk. I don't see my friends anywhere. Jason is probably in his office since he's an attorney, but Libby isn't at her desk. She's Jason's secretary. Meanwhile, I'm my worst nightmare's secretary. I've thought about getting a different job. I have applications started for at least ten of them, but I haven't submitted them. Sometimes, I dream about leaving the secretary business and baking for a living. I'd go to culinary school and have my own bakery. Thinking about bakeries makes me think of Matchmaker Baker and then leads me to think of Rocky. I blush and then shake my head.

No, I am not allowed to think about him right now.

Maybe I wouldn't want another job so badly if the partners didn't fuck me over in the worst way possible by lending me out to *her*. I was the head secretary of the entire firm. I managed everyone, and even though I'm still making the same amount of money, I was designated to help out the new attorney, who refuses to let me get back to my regular job. The partners feel sorry for her since she's so beautiful and new to law. AKA, they're fucking her and want to give her what she wants so she won't tell their wives. It doesn't matter that their office manager is collateral damage.

I get settled at my desk and boot up my computer.

"Hey, Honeybear."

I look up to find Duncan standing in front of my desk with two cups of coffee. I frown.

"Honeybear? I would prefer it if you didn't call me that in general, Duncan. And don't text me anymore. I don't want an apology."

He ignores my second comment completely and says, "But I love calling you that. It's our special name. Just like your name for me is—"

"Stop—"

"Big bear." He gives me a soft smile that makes me want to punch him.

"Can I tell Arabella you're here to bring her coffee?"

He looks down at the coffee cups and frowns. He places one down in front of me. "It's actually for you."

I look at it with disdain. "I don't think that it's appropriate for you to—"

"I think we should talk, Katie. It's been a while, and I think... I know I made the worst mistake of my life."

"I think you didn't," I say. "I think you showed your

true colors, and now that Arabella dumped you for a younger, hotter guy, you're trying to get back at her."

He scoffs. "Arabella and I had one night together. We were never a thing."

"That's not what I heard," I snap at him. "According to her, you left me for her. She's got a body of a... what did she say you said, 'goddess' while I'm like the 'Pillsbury dough boy?'"

"I never said that. She's just a jealous bitch."

"Who you cheated on me with."

"One time, it was one time! And I regret it."

"You wanted to see what it was like to fuck a skinny girl, and you did. And now what? You miss my love handles?"

"I miss more than just your body, Honeybear. I miss everything about you."

"Well, I'm not interested. You broke up with me. And now you regret it, so live with it."

He frowns as Arabella walks up to my desk and smiles at us. "I see you two seem to be mending the fence. I'm so relieved."

She's so fake. I hate her so much, but she doesn't seem to be jealous at all. She didn't have genuine feelings for my boyfriend when she fucked him. She just wanted to flex against me. It happened after I was moved to become her temporary secretary. She tried to assert her dominance over me like some animal. Afterward, she's been professional for the most part when it comes to work. Though she does shove in my face that she fucks other guys in the office and that Duncan was just one of many meaningless fucks for her. His cheating on me was nothing but his need to fuck something other than me. She also told me she never orgasmed with him and apologized to me for never getting any real satisfaction from him.

I've hated her ever since, but I try to maintain a professional relationship with her because I'm professional through and through. Well, pretty much, because the partners gave me a big bonus as an apology for forcing me to stay with her. I plan on using it towards student loans, but now, I think I'd like to spend it on a massive bowl of ice cream... Ice cream. Fuck! I need to stop thinking about Rocky.

"We're not," I try to get back into the conversation. "I was just telling Duncan he can shove his coffee down his pants and burn his dick off."

She snorts, and Duncan blushes. He's tan since he loves to lounge on the patio of his father's vacation home in Santa Monica every bright and sunny day. I always avoided it and stayed inside, which got on his nerves. He constantly critiqued how pale I was and hated how rosy my cheeks got whenever I had an emotion because it was embarrassing.

"I, um. Arabella, please let me and your secretary discuss some things." Duncan asks.

Arabella looks between us and sighs. "Whatever, she's not going to be my secretary for much longer anyway. You two might as well start discussing cases."

"What do you mean?" I look between them.

Duncan shrugs, "You'll be my secretary starting

next week. It was another thing I wanted to talk to you about."

"What! How!"

"I wanted to work with you. You're a good secretary, and you do a great job... Plus, I found out about Arabella and Marty's affair and threatened him." He avoids Arabella's gaze and gives me a shy smile like that's okay. "He's more scared of someone else revealing to his wife that he's fucking someone else than the girl going to the wife. He doesn't like witnesses."

"He wanted you close." Arabella glares at Duncan. "Whatever, you're a good secretary, and I'll miss working with you, but you're replaceable like the rest."

I glare at her as she sways her barely there hips into her office, shutting the door behind her.

I turn back to glare at Duncan. "You can't be serious. I am not going to be your secretary. I *was* your secretary, and we both agreed when we started dating that it was inappropriate. Then I got promoted, and I'm not supposed to be a secretary! I'm an office manager."

"But we're not dating anymore," he clarifies. "And Marty said he'd still pay you the same and hire someone else to manage the office."

"You are unbelievable! We are never getting back together, Duncan. Get that through your thick skull. Does all that hair gel kill brain cells?"

"Maybe if we worked together again, we could get that old spark back." He ignores my outburst.

"The spark is out, Duncan. You dumped me because I'm not thin. And I'm done having both our mothers call me and ask me to lose weight so you'd take me back."

"You're thirty, Katie. You're at an age where you should be settling down. If we get back together, we'll get married, and you won't have to work. And you'll have plenty of time to exercise and—"

"I don't need this." I shove the coffee he gave me into the trash.

"She has a boyfriend now anyway," Jason walks up to us and frowns at Duncan. "And you should be working on the Harris case, Duncan. I'm not going to ask for that file again. Get your act together."

Jason is a higher-ranking attorney than Duncan, and I love that he can always put him in his place. He's a junior partner, one of the youngest in our firm, while Duncan and Arabella are just worker bees.

"You have a boyfriend?" Duncan looks over at me with hurt in his dull brown eyes.

"I..."

Jason raises his eyebrows. "She does. He knows how to treat a lady; she doesn't have to diet to please him. Or fake it when he pleases her."

Duncan turns practically purple, and he storms away without another word.

"Jason, what are you talking about?" I whisper scream at him.

He leans down, and his face grows grave. "It happened to you, too, right?"

My jaw drops.

He nods and stands straighter. "I've never felt so full in my life in more than one way."

I sigh and place my head in my hands. "It was the most delicious orgasm I've ever had, Jase. And I don't think anything will ever compare."

"We need to do something about this. It's not right... It's bizarre, and yet—"

Libby rushes into the office, looking frazzled as she approaches my desk. She has chocolate on the corner of her lip, and I can only imagine what happened between her and her candy man.

"I need to talk to the two of you." She says with a twinkle in her eye.

"My office," Jason points to his fancy office door.

All three of us go into Jason's large and very modern office. Everything is sleek and black, but the rug is white. He doesn't allow any food in here, but I notice a hand print in the shape of icing and some crumbs on the floor.

"Oh my god, you fucked the cookie!" Libby beams widely at Jason. "Was it hot? Was he gooey?"

"Libby!" Her excitement shocks me so much that I don't know what to think. "He's partially made out of marshmallow! Smacking that bubbly ass is the fucking best... I see things got a little out of hand with your chocolate boy," Jason wiggles his eyebrows at her. "You have some chocolate right here," he points to the edge of her mouth.

She blushes. "We, uh, well, Pepper and I got

carried away before I left for work. He's just so minty. My breath is a mix of chocolate and peppermint... And fuck his peppermint stick—"

"Whoa! Too much information. You both aren't freaked out that the baked goods we bought yesterday have come to life and fucked us?" I gape at them.

How are they so calm?

"It's magic." They both say in unison.

"I'm aware, but this is not okay. We're fucking food, guys. This is weird." I plop down on Jason's leather couch.

He sighs and takes a seat next to me. "It's weirdly delicious, Katie. I don't know what to say, but I don't think I want to stop."

"We have to stop. We have to do something. We have to go back to that shop. We have to stop these guys from... having us banned from all ice cream shops in America."

"Okay, you're exaggerating. And I wouldn't be banned from an ice cream shop."

"No, you'd probably be banned from every bakery and market. Oh god! Markets!"

"Katie, calm down."

"Candy shop. Anywhere they sell candy, Libs! None of us will be allowed anywhere they sell food in general."

Libby's eyes widen.

"That's only if anyone finds out we're fucking food," Jason says. "And it's not like they're real food. They're like guys just in the shape of food."

"Do we even know if they're made?" Libby asks. "What if it's a guy that was turned into food?"

"And now he's being made to fuck us? His consent was taken from him!"

"This is getting bad. Everything you say makes me feel like a dirty, bad person." Jason shivers with disgust.

"You fucked a cookie." Libby clarifies.

"His asshole was so warm and gooey."

Libby snorts.

"What? It felt good against my dick. And the warmth of his mouth and softness."

"My candy man's dick is a thick and cool peppermint candy cane, but if feels like a real cock. It's weird, but, you know, I'm just going with it. He's Christmas-themed, so we cuddled on the couch and watched a Christmas movie together. It was amazing. He's the perfect holiday treat."

"Okay, stop!" I shout.

"Tell me you didn't have a great orgasm from a banana split," Libby asks.

"I..."

"Does he have banana fingers? Or is it a banana dick? Is it ripe before he gets hot and then reverses to being unripe? Please tell me he's not shriveled up and overripe." Jason shivers in disgust.

"He has ice cream cone fingers, and that's beside the point."

"Are they the pointed ice cream cones or—"

"Stop! I don't want to fuck a banana split now, then, or ever."

"Did he take advantage of you?" Jason's brow furrows.

"Yeah, you sound like you're not consenting. Did the ice cream rape you?" Libby's tone becomes serious.

"Ice cream rape!" Jason exclaims. "It sounds so wrong."

"He didn't rape me... He just... I just... Yes, we had sex, and he went down on me this morning, and it was... Different from anything I've ever had." I lean in toward them, and they lean into me. I whisper, "I came for the first time with someone. And you know, I never really came without help with Duncan."

They both gasp.

"Not someone, something," Libby giggles. "But I get you, girl. I've never come so hard in my life."

"Me too," Jason nods.

We all look at each other in shock before I say, "This is wrong."

"So wrong," Jason bites his lip.

"But also so right! I mean, think about it. They're the perfect boyfriends. They're great at sex, and Pepper is so sweet. This morning, he made me hot cocoa with marshmallows and Christmas-themed pancakes with red and green sprinkles. It was festive and wonderful all at once and hot. So fucking hot."

"Ginny made me gingerbread cookies for breakfast. I don't normally eat sweets during the holidays, but it was so good. It also also a little weird since, you know, he is one."

"What about you, Katie? What happened with you?"

"Well, uh..." I think about how they had such sweet moments with their dessert boyfriends and think back about Rocky. "He gave me a banana split this morning... That he pulled out from his chest."

They both gape at me.

"And he gave me an orgasm. And he... Well, I don't know."

"Did you guys talk or anything?" Jason asks.

"Pepper and I talked all night long. We had sex and talked about everything from movies we both love to music. But his favorite Christmas movie is Die Hard. He also loves rock music, somehow, and says that if he were human, he'd want to own a Christmas tree farm."

"He's perfect for you, you little Christmas fiend." Jason laughs.

"And then we had sex again, and then I took a bath because I was covered in chocolate, and then we watched a Hallmark movie and snuggled up on the couch. He even made popcorn and mixed red and green candies in it."

"Did he make the candy himself?" Jason asks. "Ginny just breaks off a piece of his body and then morphs it with his hands into a cookie. The part of his body that he broke off regenerates right away."

"Libby, your chocolate man has favorites?" I gawk. "He's made of chocolate! How does he know anything about anything?"

"He knows where the g-spot is, that's for sure," she

giggles. "And his Christmas movie knowledge is impeccable. He says he loves Halloween, too, and is just big on holidays. He knows so much about the origin of myths and stuff that created holidays that I was like, 'no way,' and he was like, 'way,' and I looked up what he said, and it was true."

"Maybe Mrs. Owens bewitches them into your dream guy or something," Jason shrugs. "Because Ginny knew is like my soulmate, sexually and emotionally, we like talked, guys. Like I really talked to a guy. And it was the best sex of my life. I'm sold on cookie sex."

"So, you guys like... talked with them? And you're okay with having food as your boyfriend?"

"I mean," they look at each other and nod.

"I always thought food was better than sex," Jason adds. "Now I have the best of both worlds."

"This is crazy! We've gone crazy! We're hopped up on some drugs." I say. "The crazy old baker probably drugged us."

"I'm not drugged, that's for sure. I know what being doped up feels like," Libby says. "And this isn't it. This is real, Katie. It's real. We have boyfriends who are food."

"Well, he's not my boyfriend," I stand up from my spot. "He's a fucking banana split!"

"Tell me, is his dick a banana? How ripe was he? Does he go from overripe to underripe when he gets turned on?" Jason asks.

I flush.

The two of them look at each other and say, "He totally does."

"Enough! I'm going to get answers. I'm not going to have a banana split for a boyfriend. I want someone to marry and take home to my parents. Can you imagine? 'Mom, Dad, this is Rocky. He's a banana split that is in the shape of a man, and he made me come so hard that I don't think I'll ever have that great of sex again. Oh, and his balls are chocolate truffles!'"

"I mean, if you're describing your boyfriend's balls in any way to your parents, it says something about your relationship with them," Jason smirks, and Libby giggles.

"Guys! Come on. This is insane."

"No, what's insane is that you haven't had a real conversation with him. What did you call him again?"

"Rocky," I avert my eyes. "Like Rocky Road Ice Cream."

"Rocky," Jason smiles kindly at me, and I want to punch him. "Why don't you go home and spend the day talking to him, getting to know him? You'll see how great it is to have a boyfriend that's perfect for you in every way, treats you right, makes you have an orgasm," he gives me a pointed look. "And he'll probably be everything you want in a man."

"I—"

"I'll tell Arabella I sent you home because you were sick of Duncan. And I'll talk with the partners about Duncan being your boss. I'll get you your job back. I got more on them than either of those shitheads."

"Okay, this is insane. I'm out of here. I have work to do—"

Jason intercoms Arabella, "Bells, honey, Katie is going to be absent today. She just got sick.... Yes, Duncan's presence did it... I know he's a bad fuck, and I agree she could do better... Yes, I know you did her a favor," he curls his lip. I close my eyes, wanting none of this to happen. "Thank you... Let's lunch never... I hate your guts bitch."

Then he hangs up the phone.

"You talk to her like that?" I'm shocked by his abrasiveness.

"She fucked over my best friend. Of course, I'm going to talk to her like that. She's stupid enough to think I'm just teasing her. I don't tell her otherwise. So, whatever. Now, go home and make nice with the banana boy—I mean Rocky."

I gaze at both of my friends' hopeful eyes and nod. "Okay. I'll go home and talk to him... But that doesn't mean I will have an ice cream boyfriend forever."

"Maybe, maybe not," Libby shrugs. "You shouldn't care what your parents think, Katie. All that matters is you're happy, and if he makes you happy, that counts."

"He makes me come."

"And that would make anyone happy," Jason is so giddy that I think he's high. "Now, go."

He waves his hand at me and then turns to Libby.

"You too. I have..." He looks at his desk drawer. "Things to do."

"Is that gingerbread man in that drawer, Jason?" Libby folds her arms and gives him a pointed glare.

Jason bites his lip.

"Okay, I'm gone. Goodbye." I leave without another word and head to my desk.

Duncan is nowhere to be seen, neither is Arabella, so I escape and sigh as I head home to my ice cream boyfriend.

five

· · ·

$\mathcal{I}$ don't know what to expect to find when I get home. Will he still be in the freezer? Will he be eating the old diet yogurt I ate close to the end of my relationship with Duncan?

What I don't expect is to find my ice cream boyfriend vacuuming my carpet and my apartment to be sparkly clean. The Christmas lights are twinkling, and the tree is in impeccable order. It's like he reorganized the decorations to ease my OCD. I even notice something new, a spoon hanging from the tree, and I blush, remembering that spoon was in my mouth this morning.

"Did you do all of this?" I look around and see that things are cleaner than they ever are when I clean. The floor sparkles and the wooden dining table is polished. My couch pillows are fluffed, and my TV speakers play "All I Want for Christmas is You" by the Queen of Christmas.

"Do you... Like Mariah?" I gape at him.

He jumps and holds his ice cream cone fingers over where a human heart would be.

"Shit, you scared me." He goes to the stereo and turns off the music before walking over to me and pulling me into his arms. I gasp as he dips me and presses a chilly, gooey kiss to my lips. He tastes like vanilla mixed with cherry, and I take a soft bite out of his lip. He moans as ice cream melts in my mouth. He pulls away and I notice a sprinkle and some ice cream is missing from his lips before it regenerates like I didn't just bite a piece of ice cream off him. "I'm happy you're home."

"Me too," I lick the sweet vanilla taste off my lips.

He pulls me into a standing position, and I say, "So, uh... Mariah Carey?"

"Ah, yes." He says. "I've always been a fan—also Taylor Swift. You have her new albums framed on your wall behind the tree. Why would you put the tree in front of them?"

"My sister isn't a fan, and she set up the decorations. But that's beside the point, how do you like music? You're ice cream, and Mrs. Owens made you like the day we met, right? Unless..." My stomach churns. "Someone has taken a bite of you before."

He laughs. "No one has eaten me before, baby. You're the first. And the last. I was made for you."

"So, what, when I bought you, you just like were bewitched to know all about me?"

He frowns. "That's not really how it works."

I'm about to ask how it works when he pulls me to the couch and plops down, pulling me onto his lap.

"If you want to know more about me, I'll tell you. I love Taylor Swift's music, and Mariah Carey's Christmas Music always plays in the shop. It gets stuck in my head, and even when I don't want to think about it, I do. I like basketball and football and wish I could play them soon. I love comedy, action, and superhero movies. My favorite film is Don't Tell Mom The Babysitter's Dead."

"A classic, but how?"

He doesn't answer as he continues. "I love coffee-flavored things, like you, but I can't have hot coffee. I like coffee-flavored almond fro-yo. And most of all, I've been waiting my whole life for someone like you to enter it. Someone who is a lot like me."

"You were made like yesterday. And most of those things are things I like."

"It's a sheer coincidence."

"Or she made you in my image," I mutter. "I'm not a fan of Basketball, though. I like Hockey."

"Like the hockey romances you read?" He smirks.

My jaw drops. "How did you—"

"I may have snooped around and found your Kindle. But don't get the thought into your head that I liked everything I said, so you'd like me back. It's all true."

I look him up and down. "Well, you're my dream man in ice cream form, right?"

He smiles brightly, and I notice his teeth are white

sprinkles cut to look like perfect straight teeth. "I also love banana splits."

"So, we like pretty much all the same things?"

"Yes." He says. "We do."

"Except for, like, basketball and stuff..."

"Well, I have to differ from you somehow. No one is perfect, not even ice cream."

I almost say that he is perfect, then shake my head.

"So, you cleaned today? How is that even possible when you're ice cream? I'm shocked nothing is sticky."

"I'm talented like that. Now, what would you like to do? I'm assuming they gave you the day off for some reason—are you sick? Did something happen?"

I open my mouth to dismiss it all, but instead, I say, "My ex manipulated his way into being my new boss because he wants me back."

He growls. "And you don't want him back, right?"

"I don't. The guy says he loves me and wants me. He said that breaking up was the worst mistake of his life, yet he still says it's not a big deal for me to drop a few pounds. He cheated on me too... With my current boss. She likes to throw it in my face how bad a fuck he is and acts like she pities me for being with him for years. He also did it right around Halloween when I was looking at couples' costumes. Then they showed up to the company Halloween party together, looking like some model and a billionaire. She dumped him soon after. She tries to suggest places where I can get a good lay and also sex toys that would help me orgasm since I probably never did with Duncan."

"That's horrible."

"I think she's just stupid. She likes to show that she's powerful, but she's also not smart about it. She likes to think she's a big deal, but she was such a mess that the partners wanted me to help her out. I'm the office manager and was the top secretary for a long time. It was supposed to be temporary that I help her and find her the perfect secretary match. She wasn't pleased to learn that I wasn't going to be her secretary for long and thought I thought I was too good to be her secretary, so she fucked my boyfriend to show that she was better than me. He broke up with me soon after, and then I learned everything from her. And Halloween happened. Of course, she's rejected and scared away every secretary they send her, so I've been stuck with her. Then Duncan talked to the partners and got me to be his secretary."

"That sounds epically horrible! Do you want me to fight the asshole? Or the bitch? I can worm my way into her system and give her diabetes."

"That is a little intense," I say.

"I can also fight your ex. I can make my fists into hard candy, and it's not like he can hurt me."

"Also, no."

"I'm sorry. I hate that they did that to you. I'd never do that to you. I want you to feel like a princess every day we're together. I want to cherish you, make you happy, and satisfy your needs."

"I think..." I look into his gumdrop eyes, and I don't

know why, but they're so soft and make my heart melt. "That would be nice."

"You could use a little TLC, and I'll give it to you, baby. But first," he says as he flips me onto my back on the couch. "I think we should get a few things straight." He hovers over me.

"Like what?" My heart races, and his cold, sweet touch melts my heart as he drags his soft finger against my cheek.

"I don't want you working with Duncan. Or at that place much longer."

I laugh. "As you can see, I need the money. I have so much student loan debt and credit card debt—"

"Shhh," he holds up his waffle cone finger to my lips, and he smells different today like sweet caramel has been drizzled all over his body. I lick my lips. "I will take care of everything."

"You're an ice cream man. You can't make money. How—"

"Don't worry so much." He presses his lips to mine, and I gasp as his hand moves to my breast and he rolls a nipple between his rough, ridged fingers. His touch is rougher and more forceful than before, like he's taking out his rage on my body from hearing about my ex. I kind of like it. It's just the right amount of salt to make me crave more of his sweetness.

I can't help myself but want to feel him. I move my hand down his body until I push it into his ice cream surface and feel his hard, unripe banana dick against my palm. It's curved but not in too crazy of a way, and he growls as I stroke him from his icy pelvis to the tip of the banana. A drop of hot caramel leaks from his tip, and I moan, thinking about how sweet and salty that will taste.

"Are you hungry for my banana, baby?"

"Mmm," I say as he moves quickly, shifting us so I'm straddling his lap. I'm still holding his banana, and he bites down on my nipple. I feel prickles of sprinkles nipping at my flesh through my shirt.

I taste sugar in the air. It's a mix of vanilla, fudge, and caramel. I want him so bad, and I don't know if I'll last long. I shift my body off of him and kneel before him as he spreads his creamy legs. His big banana dick is on full display, and I notice the tip is covered in hot gooey caramel mixed with fudge. I lick my lips and take the tip of him into my mouth. I swirl my tongue around his fruity head before I lick down his banana cock to his truffled balls. I lick them, and he sucks in a deep breath. He's so sweet and salty I want more. I move my mouth back over the top of him and take his whole length in my mouth.

"Fuck, baby." He mutters. "You suck like you're tasting a frozen chocolate-covered banana."

Bursts of flavors assault my senses. He tastes like banana candy covered in cream. He moans and grabs my hair as he shoves my head down his whole length. I choke on him and feel tears prick my eyes as he moves my head up and down him. The mixture of his fudge caramel precum and his banana flavor overwhelm me, and I nearly lose myself and bite into him. I don't, though, because I want that mix of flavor to shoot down my throat as I hear him reach the same amount of ecstasy as I did when he fucked me last night and made me come this morning.

Suddenly he moves my head up and down faster, and I swirl my tongue around the head of his delectable cock. He grunts as a mixture of sweet and salty hits the back of my throat. His hot fudge and salted caramel syrup shoot down my throat, and I swallow all the sugary goodness. I pull away and watch as more liquid shoots out of him like someone squeezing a bottle of syrup. It hits my shirt and my face. Once he's done and tries to catch his breath, I lick the chocolate off my lips and then look at his chocolate-covered banana. I bend down and lick down his shaft, lapping up any last trace of decadence there is.

"Jeez, baby, you're going to make me come again before I even had a chance to rest." He chuckles but squirms under my lips.

I pull away from him and take my finger to remove some stray caramel syrup from the edge of my lip before putting it in my mouth and lapping the remainder of his tasty cum. "You taste so delicious I almost bit your dick off."

He laughs. "Never thought I'd hear that one."

I roll my eyes. "You're new to this world. You haven't heard any of them."

He gives me a small smile. "True. But still. Being brought to life with a banana for a dick was not something anyone expects."

"I don't think anyone is born with a banana dick."

"I was."

I sit beside him on the couch, pick up the remote, and ask, "What movie are you interested in watching? Any action movies or comedies?"

"I know you hate Christmas, but this room makes me feel festive." I frown at his response.

"Do you mind if we watch... Elf? I love Will Ferrell." He pulls me against him, and I cuddle into his chilly embrace.

"Don't tell anyone, but I love that movie... And" I glance around my apartment. My body warms, but not in a way that would melt Rocky. I smile, feeling some of that Christmas cheer I used to love. "I'm feeling in the Christmas spirit too."

six

· · ·

The next morning, I wake up knowing I have the day off because it's Saturday. Rocky and I had sex all night long, and it was the most delicious thing that's ever been done to my body.

I don't think I can get enough of him, and to be honest, I don't want to get enough of him, and that's what leads me to sneak out of my apartment while he's in the freezer and drive myself to the bakery where he was made.

The shop is open but not busy, which is a plus for me. I walk into the bakery and spot Mrs. Owens behind the register. She's looking at something on her phone. I don't expect a witch to rely on technology like that, but whatever.

"Mrs. Owens," I say.

She jumps and places a hand over her ample chest. "Oh, heavens dear, you scared me. Oh! I know you;

you're ice cream boyfriend, girl. How can I help you today? Are you enjoying your ice cream surprise?"

"Ice Cream Surprise is something to call him, I guess." I cross my arms and start tapping my feet. "You bewitched an ice cream and made it seduce me. What the hell?"

She waves her hand in the air. "Oh, please, like you aren't enjoying him."

"What Rocky and I do is none of your business."

"Rocky," she smirks at the name.

I feel my cheeks flush and stammer, "W-what you do is wrong! Preying on single women and men and giving them food as boyfriends is not a nice thing to do."

"How so?"

"Well, I..." I don't know what to say. I don't know why I came down here, but I needed to say my peace and make this woman know that what she did was wrong. "I don't want an ice cream boyfriend! I want a real human boyfriend. Ice cream is food. It's not right."

"Who cares? It's not like you introduced him to your parents." She snorts.

"That's the thing! I can't introduce him to my parents! Rocky is sweet and charming, he gives me the best pleasure I've ever experienced, and I am starting to fall for a fucking banana split! This is not the kind of life I want. I want a family. I want a husband and kids, and I want to introduce my boyfriend to my parents and not have some secret fucked up relationship with food."

"There's nothing wrong with loving food."

"You make me want to go on an actual diet!"

I feel tears prick my eyes. Maybe Duncan was right. Maybe I should lose weight. Maybe it's the fact that I eat so many sweets and things that this is some karma.

"Oh, honey, don't cry." She walks around the counter and pulls me into her arms. She's warm and comfortable and smells like sugar. "You don't need a diet. And I'm sorry about falling in love with something you don't want. My goal is to make people happy. I'm a witch who loves to match-make. But there aren't a lot of people who approach matchmakers... I thought that by doing this, I would be helping others out."

"I... I want to be happy but real happy, not fake happy like I was with Duncan." I sniff.

"I think you are real happy. You don't realize that sometimes unexpected things can make us happy."

She pulls away from me and looks at my tear-soaked face.

"Here, I'll help you out. If you are unhappy with your ice cream boyfriend and want to break up with him, there's an incantation you can use that will make him turn into a real piece of food that doesn't come to life. He'll never become a talking, walking, best sex ever, real guy again. He'll be ice cream. You can eat him, throw him out, do whatever you want, and then you can move on with your life."

The concept makes my heart ache at the very thought, but I know deep down that this is what I need.

Who cares what I want? I *need* a real relationship with a human.

"What's the incantation?"

She sighs. "I hate sugar."

My eyebrows shoot up. "That's it? That's all."

"Also, sugar gives me a toothache, or I can't stomach sugar. Stuff about hating sugar will make them drop dead."

"Drop dead? Like, kill him?"

"That's what you're doing, yes. You're killing his essence and making him into an average banana split. Never to touch you again."

I bite my lip and nod.

"Your friends are right, Katie. You are a bah-humbug."

I don't know how she knows they call me that, but I don't bother listening to anything more. I leave the bakery and cry on my car ride home. Can I do this to Rocky?

I stop my car in my parking spot and shake my head. "No. I'm not going to kill my ice cream boyfriend. Rocky is the best guy I've ever met. He's made me happy in more ways than I ever imagined. He accepts my body and makes me feel beautiful. He's delicious, too, in so many ways that I can't imagine life without him. Who cares if I don't take him home to see my shitty family? So what if I can't have kids? That's not everything in life. If I can come home to a banana split daily for the rest of my life, I think I'd be the happiest woman in the world."

Get out of my car with a new view of the world and life. I will stay with my ice cream boyfriend until my life is over and he melts away with me.

seven

. . .

I head up to my apartment and stop mid-step when I notice Duncan outside the door. He's sitting on the floor, legs out with a half-drunk bottle of wine in his hand and an ugly bouquet of various shades of roses in the other.

"Duncan, what are you doing here?"

"Jason told me you had a new boyfriend, so I came here to fight the fucker." He snaps. "But I don't have the courage to go in and fight him, honey bear."

I roll my eyes. He's always been a weak little shit.

He carries on, "I love you, honey bear. Please come back to me. I'll make you happy. You don't have to lose a single pound. I'll never fuck anyone else as long as I live. You have the right to cut off my balls if I do."

"That implies you might do it."

"I won't! I swear. I love you and your love handles and chubby stomach."

"Okay, you need to stop."

"I love that you have that big fat ass, and those tits—"

"Duncan, you're drunk. And you've called me fat like twice in the last minute. I think you need to leave. I'll get you an Uber or something."

"No!" He says, throwing the bottle aside. It crashes to the floor, causing the glass to shatter everywhere and the remaining wine to stain the hallway carpet.

"Fuck." I scrub my face with my hands. "You need to leave now."

"Please take me back. I love you. I'm sorry for what I told all those guys about your body and that I tried to make you lose weight."

"Stop! And who did you tell about my body?"

"I... Well, some of the guys were talking after work about how hot your curves were, so I told them about your stretch marks and your cellulite. I didn't want them getting any ideas."

"You fucking bastard," I slap him across the face.

"Um, ow." He holds his face with his hand. "That hurt, honey bear."

"Don't honey bear me, Duncan!"

I get up from the floor and head to my door. He jumps up just as I unlock the door. I open it, and he pushes the door open from behind me, making us both spill into the room.

"Get off me!" He lays on top of me. He moans like he's the one that got hurt.

"I'm so sorry, honey bear."

"Duncan! Get the fuck off me!" I scream.

He starts touching my body, grabbing onto my hips. "You feel so good. What was I thinking about letting you go? I love these hips. They're perfect to grab!"

"I said stop!" I try to buck him off me, but he moans as his tiny dick nudges my back.

"What the fuck is going on here?" Rocky shouts, and Duncan stops what he's doing. This allows me to shove him off me, and Rocky helps me into a standing position.

"I must be fucking drunk because a banana split is talking to me," Duncan says.

I look at Rocky and then look at Duncan. "You... You are drunk. Super drunk. This is my boyfriend, and he's not a banana split. He's a real-life person. And you need to leave now before he kicks your ass."

"But, honey bear—"

Rocky grabs Duncan by the collar, ice cream drips onto my ex-boyfriend's body, and I take a moment to watch as Duncan's eyes widen, and he screams like a little girl. "Holy shit! It's an ice cream monster!"

He pushes himself away from Rocky and runs screaming out of my building. I shove the door closed and turn to glare at Rocky. "What the fuck do you think you were doing showing yourself to him?"

"What do you mean? What were you doing letting him touch you like that? Or come into the apartment at all!"

"I didn't. I was trying to get in, and he attacked me!"

"Attacked you!" He mutters a curse. "I should kill him. Absorb him into my cream and drown him."

"That's a disturbing image. And no, you shouldn't!"

"Where were you today? I woke up in the freezer, came out, and you were nowhere in sight."

I look at him in shock. Fuck, what do I tell him? Suddenly, my phone rings, and I pull it from my purse. My mother's number and face beams at me.

"That's my mom—"

"Katie, we're not done—"

"Hi, Mom," I hold up my hand to Rocky.

"Is this a bad time, sweetie-pie? You sound flustered."

"It's not a bad time."

"Oh," she sounds down. "I was hoping that you would say it was and you were with your new boyfriend."

"New boyfriend?"

"Yes! I called you earlier, but you didn't answer, and then I tried to video chat with you. The camera was off, but your new boyfriend Rocco was on the phone, and we chatted."

"My new boyfriend?" I glare at Rocky.

He's smiling like he's won a prize.

"Yes! Of course, he's so sweet. I love him already. He even talked about joining us for Christmas! I thought you weren't coming. Now I'll have to make up your room. Your father will want him to sleep in the guest room, but I'll talk to him. You have a queen-sized bed, after all."

"The holidays!" I feel my stomach drop.

"I'm thinking of a winter wedding. He said he likes the cold."

"He likes the cold." I feel my world crashing down around me.

"Why are you repeating everything I'm telling you?"

"Because I uh... Mom, can I call you back?" My rage starts to boil, and I know if he comes near me, I'll melt his fucking face off.

"Of course, dear. But next time, answer your video calls with him. I want to see what he looks like. He sounds so delicious!"

I cringe at her description. "Oh, he is."

"Goodbye, honey!"

She hangs up, and I scowl at Rocky. "You spoke to my mother?"

"She called, and I wanted to make her happy and let her know you were being taken care of."

"A winter wedding?" I feel my blood heat. I laugh cruelly. "And coming home for the holidays? Please explain to me, Rocky, how I tell my mother that my boyfriend is ice cream!"

"Some women have fake big teddy bears for boyfriends. You have a talking ice cream. Don't worry, I won't let her taste me." He gives me a cocky grin.

"That's not the fucking point!" I throw my arms up in the air in frustration.

"So you want her to taste me?"

"Rocky! Stop it! This is serious. You're an ice cream man! You're not even a human! You don't have a real heart or a real anything. You're made of milk and sugar! I can't marry milk and sugar! I love ice cream, but—"

"But not that much?" He sounds angry. "I know that's what you were going to say. You love ice cream, but not this way. It's lies. You love my ice cream. You'd eat it daily for the rest of your life if you could! Don't deny it."

"I am denying it! I want a real life. Not some fantastical magic-filled one. I want to get married, go on vacations, have kids, and grow old with someone. I want to spend Christmas ice skating, picking out Christmas trees, shopping for decorations, and drinking eggnog. I want to visit New York and get married somewhere in a winter wonderland."

"There's eggnog fro-yo." He adds.

"I don't want to give that up for an ice cream man that can't give me a real life!"

"Who says I can't? We could try for a little sundae! We could get married in a winter wonderland in New York where we can go ice skating! Christmas is snowy! We can elope this Christmas even and do it now! You seem not to want your family there, so why not?"

"Think about what people will say and think!"

"You care so much about what others think, don't you? About how they perceive your body or your relationship with Duncan. When your friends call you a bah-humbug, you want to cry and shout that you love Christmas, but it's hard when there's no one to share it with. You can share it with me, damn it! You can have a life with me. I love your body, every curve. I want to cover you with my cream. I want to make little sundaes with you and grow old."

"I'm not marrying an icy dessert!"

"The only icy thing in here is you!"

"Well, you know what, Rocky, milk spoils and has an expiration date! And yours is now."

"What—"

"I hate sugar!" I scream.

Rocky's eyes widen, and his whole body shakes. Realizing what I just said hits me, I start shaking in fear. "No... No. I didn't mean that. I didn't—"

"Too late," his voice is hoarse. "I love you... Katie."

"No!"

Suddenly, Rocky freezes solid and begins to shrink. Tears rain down my face as I watch his body become a bowl of ice cream, and abruptly, it starts to melt.

"No, no! I love you. I love you! Don't leave me. Rocky!"

I sob so hard as I watch the bananas ripen and grow mold. His ice cream cone fingers grow soggy, and his cherry nose shrivels up. I watch his fudge hair melt with the ice cream, creating a sticky, milky puddle in the bowl.

What have I done?

eight

. . .

$\mathcal{A}$ few days passed, and I couldn't even look at ice cream. I called in sick to work but didn't tell my friends about what I did. I told Jason, who got my job back that I needed some time off. He said, "Okay, wink wink," thinking no doubt that Rocky and I were getting up to no good. Only Rocky and I weren't getting up to anything. He's dead. He's melted, and all that's left is a bowl with Matchmaker Baker's logo on it and a spoon. They're the exact ones he'd pulled from his chest to feed me with. I can't help but think that maybe it was all a dream. I'll wake up tomorrow, and I can pretend that none of this ever happened.

Instead of going straight to my comfort food, ice cream, I eat salty popcorn and chips. I sit in front of the TV and watch a horror movie, the furthest thing from anything Christmas and happy. Of course, I pick a fucking movie that's based in December and has

Krampus as the villain. I feel Krampus. I mean, I don't, but I hate fucking Christmas, and it's jolly-ness and the free stuff you get at bakeries because they feel bad for you. After all, you're a depressed loser, and your friends are scared you'll become one of those depressed holiday suicides you hear about. I don't want to die, but thinking of what I did to Rocky makes me feel like I deserve to.

I got a text from Duncan asking if I was okay and that he had the most crazy dream. I don't bother to respond. I don't even respond to my sister or mom regarding anything. Not even when they both text me to tell me my sister's wedding is off because my sister's shithead fiance cheated on her with his best friend's wife. Just as I'm about to go back to bed and cry, my doorbell rings, and I drag myself to it. I don't bother looking into the peephole because if it's a serial killer, who cares? I'm a murderer, too. I murdered my boyfriend because we fought over something so stupid.

"Katie?" My younger sister Krissy says as she stands in my doorway with a suitcase and backpack. Krissy is curvy like me, but not as curvy, making it so mom didn't give her too hard of a time lately because she lost weight for her wedding. She has the same shade of blonde hair as me, blue eyes, and fair skin. Her hair is in a knot on her head, and her eyes look tired.

"Krissy, what are you doing here?"

"I needed a break from Mom and Chad. He's been

calling nonstop to get the wedding going again, and Mom isn't helping. I decided to run away from home..."

"Come on in," I move out of the way to let her into my apartment. She looks around, and her jaw drops. "I know, it's a mess. I haven't been well lately, so I haven't felt the need to clean up."

"All my Christmas decorations..." tears well in her eyes.

The first thing I did after Rocky melted was tear down the Christmas decorations and throw them all in the garbage. I did save our childhood ornaments, but other than that, I wanted nothing Christmas in my apartment. I even removed the Mariah Carey Christmas poster I put up yearly for the holidays. I deleted Christmas songs from my playlists, too. I didn't delete Taylor Swift, but I am listening to more of her break-up songs.

"I'm sorry," I say. "I wasn't in a good place."

"This is... Well, it's okay."

I look at the rest of my apartment and wonder how it got messy. When did I order pizza? Did I eat the whole thing and leave the box on the table? I slowly sniff my clothes and cringe. I haven't showered in over twenty-four hours, yet I reek of a sad, lonely girl who is too tired to live.

"I can clean off the couch, and you could sleep there for now. It's a futon, technically."

She gives me a small smile, but I know it's pitying. "That would be... nice. Thanks."

She places her backpack on my dining room chair and drops her suitcase close to the front door.

"So, is this about Duncan?" She asks.

I scoff. "Duncan is a thing of the past. This I about..." I can't say his name, but I force myself. I was ashamed of my ice cream boyfriend; now he's melted. I should have just gone with it and accepted who and what he was. I should have married him at Christmas and tried to have sundae babies. "His name was Rocky, and he melted my heart."

"Melted your heart. That sounds intense."

"I melted him," I sob.

"Hey, it's okay." she pulls me to the couch, where we both sit. "Mom said you were dating someone new, but it's already over?"

"He's... He's dead!" I cry, and she gasps.

She opens her arms to me, and I fall into them.

Krissy lets me cry and ramble about everything that happened. When she looks at me like I'm crazy, I go to the bowl Rocky left behind and hand it to her. "This was his," I say.

"A bowl and spoon?" She lifts her brow.

"I know, it's crazy, and I don't know what... But I don't think I'll ever get over him. He was the perfect man."

"There's no such thing as perfect. He sounds like he was clingy and needy."

"He was! But I liked that about him. I would have agreed to a Christmas wedding if he were a human.

Fuck, I'd agree to if he was here and still a banana split. I'd have his sundae babies."

"You said that a few times now. I don't think that's how anything works, Katie. But, like, what the fuck are you doing here, Katie!"

"I know you think I'm crazy—"

"No! I mean, what are you doing just sitting here crying? Do you want your man? You should get him back! Go back to that witch and get your boyfriend back. She could make him again, couldn't she? She could make you another ice cream boyfriend that's the same."

"It will never be the same."

"You don't know that!" Krissy snaps as she stands abruptly and pulls me up from the couch. "Get dressed. Look hot and beautiful. We're going to get your ice cream boyfriend back."

"I don't know about that, Krissy. I just..."

"No, we're doing it, and you won't be sorry. You deserve your happily ever after, and who cares if it's with ice cream? And you should not tell your friends about how he died. They love their dessert men, and after seeing the way you are, I would hate for them to feel the same way."

"Okay."

"Now scoot!" she pats me on the butt.

"You're just doing this to get yourself an ice cream boyfriend, right?"

"Most definitely! Chad never gave me a good orgasm. I always had to get myself off. I'm ready for some dessert, man, to make my day. Maybe a popsicle or a cupcake!"

I think of Rocky's popsicle and bite my lip.

"Okay," I say with renewed determination. "I'm going to get Rocky back."

nine

. . .

"I'm sorry, honey, but you can't get Rocky back." Mrs. Owens says as she gives me pitying eyes.

My sister is busy looking at the displays of cupcake men, and she has her eye on a strawberry cake that seems vaguely familiar.

"But, he's my soulmate. I love him!"

"He's dead, Katie. I'm sorry, there are no refunds or returns. Once you say those words, he's no more."

"I just," my eyes fill with tears. "I loved him so much. He was my world. I said stupid things because I was mad and shouldn't have. I regret it and will regret it the rest of my life."

She sighs. "I wish there were something I could do for you, but there isn't."

I nod, and all the hope I had coming into the bakery vanishes.

"I would like this one, please." Krissy points to the

strawberry cupcake. "He looks like my ex's best friend."

"Interesting choice," Mrs. Owens says.

"Yeah, his wife and my fiance were banging, and it ruined our lives. Sadly, we hate each other, but maybe I can get some of that pent-up sexual frustration we've had since high school out of the way with a cupcake that looks like him."

Mrs. Owens snorts and nods, ringing my sister up.

"Maybe you'd like to see some other options, dear," Mrs. Owens asks. "It's not the first time someone didn't like their match."

"But I loved him!" I snap, and a few lunch patrons look at me. The place isn't too crowded, but I feel embarrassed that I've thrown a tantrum.

"Just think about it." She gives me a pitying look and tears well in my eyes.

We leave the bakery, my sister with her new boyfriend and me alone. Krissy suggests she go to a hotel to have some "alone time" with her cupcake, and I remind her to wait until tomorrow and that tonight might be one of the best of her life.

Once she leaves, I curl up on my couch and cry myself to sleep.

ten

. . .

*I*t's been two weeks since Rocky died. That's what I call it. Died. Murdered. I murdered my boyfriend.

I should go to the police and turn myself in, but he was a fucking ice cream. I'd be institutionalized.

I go to my favorite coffee shop before work and sit at a table while drinking a peppermint mocha latte. I'm in a daze when I get up, throw out my cup, and head to the door, only to run into someone. I cry out as I begin to fall to the floor when two big hands grab hold of my arms and help steady me.

I look up into my savior's eyes and find two sparkling blue eyes looking at me with concern. My mouth gapes open as I notice the similarities between this human stranger and my Rocky.

"Rocky?" I mutter.

"Are you okay, Miss?" He says in a voice so similar to the ice cream I love.

"Um, yes. Sorry," I shake myself out of my trance. The guy smirks at me just like Rocky did, but where his ice cream had vague dimples, this guy has real dimples and they light up his face. My cheeks flush. "I was zoned out."

"It's alright. Here, do you need to sit for a moment? You look like you've seen a ghost."

I nod to him in utter shock. How could this be? Did Mrs. Owens make Rocky in this guy's image? Rage slithers over me at the thought of that witch bitch.

"Hold on a sec." He goes over to the register, and I watch him as he orders his coffee and then asks for a cup of water. He pays and then walks over to me with the water.

"Here, drink this," I take the cup from his hand and sip it slowly.

"Thank you," I say.

"No problem. You look so familiar." He says.

"I—"

"Sorry," He has fair skin, dark black hair, blue eyes, and pink lips. He's tall and muscular and looks good enough to eat—Okay, I need to stop that. He's human. I'm not going to eat this human man.

"It's okay," I say. "You look familiar, too."

"I feel like we've met before." He says.

"Maybe in a dream." I laugh awkwardly.

He smiles at me so sweetly. His teeth are straight and not made of sprinkles, but he's so gorgeous that I try not to compare them.

"Do you usually zone out like that?"

I shake my head. "It's a first. I've been a little tired lately. Bad breakup."

He nods. "I get that. I broke up with my fiance a few months ago."

"My boyfriend dumped me because I'm fat." I blurt out and then cover my mouth.

"That guy is a shithead." He shakes his head in disgust. "You're not fat. You're beautiful."

His eyebrows shoot up, and his face turns ruddy. I can tell his expressions easily, unlike Rocky's.

"What's your story?" I ask and then want to smack myself because it's so invasive.

He doesn't seem to mind as he answers. "She cheated on me with some Patrickass. Broke my heart."

I nod.

"I don't mean to be so forward, but... Do you by any chance—would you like to go on a date? I feel a connection with you. I can't explain it."

I want to say I can. Mrs. Owens may have noticed this guy and decided to use his essence or whatever to create Rocky. Though I know it's probably wrong to do it, I say, "That would be great."

"How about we meet here, say tonight at seven? There's this wonderful Chinese restaurant a few doors down, and I'd love to take you out—" His eyes widen. "I mean, it's a great place, and I don't know why, but I think you'll like it. By the way... Shit, I should have said this before and asked you for yours. My name is Alex."

"I'm Katie."

I feel uncomfortable knowing his draw to me probably has something to do with my ice cream man... but I agree to meet him anyway. We exchange numbers just in case one of us will be late, and I nibble on my lip as I tell him I have to go to work.

He smiles and waves as I leave the coffee shop.

Even though I sense this is wrong, part of me feels it's just right.

eleven

· · ·

*A*lex and I have been dating for a few weeks now, and we haven't had sex yet. I don't know if he's waiting for the right moment or if it's me. Every time he kisses me goodnight, I'm so close to asking him in, but the thought of Rocky keeps me from doing it. His bowl and spoon still sit on my kitchen counter. But today, I put it away and decided it's time I moved on. Rocky was just an ice cream man. Alex is the real deal, and I'm really and truly falling for him. I don't know how I can be in love with two men at once... Well, a man and ice cream. But my heart is torn in two.

It's Christmas Eve, and after my hatred for Christmas everything, I decided to say, fuck it. I bought a new tree, smaller and not silver, and used my old childhood decorations that Krissy brought over. I created my own Christmas wonderland in my apartment. I made a ham for dinner with all the fixings, stuffing, yams, and fruit cake. My fruit cake is good, but

I did not use any bananas. I couldn't bring myself to use it.

While I didn't want to go home and watch the shit-storm, that is, my parents give Krissy a hard time now that she's broken up with Chad. She insisted she could handle it all by herself now that she had the confidence to stand her ground. Alex mentioned his family had gone out of town, and he'd be home alone for the holidays. I was nervous but invited him and said I'd cook him dinner.

He said, "As long as there's ice cream for dessert."

I froze at that but nodded. I bought some, and without thinking, I didn't even realize I bought all the toppings for a banana split. I even bought multiple bananas and waffle cones.

I'm so gross.

I told myself I could never look at another banana split again, but when I think of Alex, I can't help but want to cover him in ice cream and lick him clean.

I blush as I finish mixing the salad, just thinking about it.

"All I Want For Christmas" by Mariah Carey plays through my apartment, and I try not to think about Rocky even more.

"No," I shake my head. "This is so wrong, it's completely inappropriately wrong. I do not want to make my boyfriend into an ice cream. He's just a normal human guy. A normal human. That's all."

I dressed in a tight green velvet dress that covered

my crotchless black panties and see-through black bra. Everything is lacy, and I'm hoping tonight is the night.

So, when my doorbell rings, I jump, and my pussy pulses at the thought of sex. It's been weeks and, before Rocky, months. But I know that I had the best sex of my life with Rocky. Alex has a tough act to follow.

I go to my door, open it, and smile at Alex, who is in jeans and a Christmas Sweater with a Christmas tree made of ice cream stitched onto it. He looks so comfortable and relaxed, and when he looks at me, his eyes widen, and I can see them darken with lust.

"You look—"

"The dress is a little tight," I bite my lip, self-conscious.

"I was going to say good enough to eat."

I step back and let him into the house, closing the door and feeling my nipples pebble at his words.

Tonight is a go!

And I know I'm right because when I turn toward Alex, he attacks me with his mouth. I gasp as his lips slam against mine, and one arm wraps around the back of my head, tugging on my hair, while the other moves to my ass and grabs me. I moan and open my mouth to him. He dips his tongue in and tastes me. He always tastes like sugar and coffee when I kiss him. My whole body lights up like a Christmas tree with need.

I revel in his touch as he angles my head so he can consume my mouth. His hand grabs my ass cheek, and he presses his body against me. I can feel his hard cock against my belly, and I move my hand toward his pants, palming him.

He groans and pulls away before saying with a panted breath, "Do you have the ice cream?"

I don't even flinch as I say, "Yes."

"Good," He pulls away from me, and like he knows where everything is in my apartment, he goes to my freezer and takes out the vanilla ice cream I bought. He opens the fridge, takes out a can of whipped cream he asked me to get and then turns back to me. "Bedroom?"

I point to my bedroom, and as he makes his way there, he has a little smile that I don't think he knows I see. He's gorgeous, and I clench my thighs together as I lead him to my room.

Once inside, I sit on my bed and watch him place the ice cream and a spoon on my dresser before taking the whipped cream and squirting some into his mouth.

"I love sweets, do you?" He asks. "I don't understand why some people don't put whipped cream on their ice cream. I prefer it."

"Me too," I don't know what I'm saying as I watch his hungry gaze take me in.

"Take off your dress. I want to see you. All of you."

I slowly lift my dress over my body and reveal myself to him. He hisses as he sucks in a breath and says, "Fuck you're gorgeous. Just like I remember?"

"What?" I ask.

"Nothing," he says.

I'm too consumed with the look he's giving me to even think about anything other than wanting him inside me. He walks toward me with the whipped cream bottle and then growls, "Bra, off, now. I want to cover you in this cream and lick it off your tits."

He's talking dirtier than Rocky ever did, and I like it. I take off my bra and reveal my breasts to him. Then he's on me. He pushes me back onto the bed and sprays the whipped cream onto each of my nipples. He throws the can to the side and sucks a bud into his mouth. I cry out as he twirls his tongue around me, and I arch into him.

My eyes close briefly, and his tongue turns from warm to ice cold, and it hardens as it twirls around my sensitive body. I shiver with anticipation.

Even when he pulls away and moves to the other breast, I still feel wet and sticky, like it's Rocky sucking me and not a human. Like his cream had dripped onto my breast.

I soak in Alex's touch as it becomes chilly. His fingers shift into ice cream cones, and one dips over my nipple, sucking it into the cone and closing up, pinching it, creating pain with this delicious pleasure.

"That's it, baby, just how I like you. I can't wait to have you again." He growls in my ear.

Again?

My eyes burst open, and it's not Alex that's pressing his human cock against my center, but Rocky's thick and unripe banana!

I scream, and Rocky jumps, sitting back. "What's wrong?" He asks, then looks down at his body and says, "Uh-oh."

"Rocky?" I whisper. "Is this a dream? Is it... Is it you?"

"My name is Alex." He says. "And yeah, it's me, baby."

My eyes widen. "But Alex is a human. He's a normal human. Not a man made of ice cream."

"I am a normal human." He sounds so guilty saying it.

"No, you're an ice cream man."

His gum-drop eyes make my whole body squirm.

"I'm both. I... I. Well, it's a long story."

"Tell me. Tell me now what the fuck is going on. How are you an ice cream man and a normal human."

He sighs and sits back. His human clothes are on the floor next to my dress, and I watch as the ice cream melts off his body.

"No!" I scream before he turns back into Alex, my normal human boyfriend.

"Well, I guess it's good to be honest with you. I was going to tell you, I just... I wanted to fuck you so badly. I've wanted to tell you everything since we met with me in this form, but I was so nervous and scared you'd freak out or not believe me. And I wanted you to fall for me, Alex, not just Rocky."

"I have fallen for Alex," I say. "And Rocky."

His blue eyes look hopeful. "Really?"

"Tell me what's going on." I don't know why my voice is soft, but I'm hopeful.

"When my fiancé Amanda cheated on me, I was lost. I discovered Mrs. Owens's shop. The Matchmaker

Baker was something I heard about through a few friends and wanted to check it out. They said they met their girlfriends and wives through it. I went inside and looked around. She asked me what was wrong, and I told her I just wanted a girlfriend who would love me for me. She told me she was a matchmaker, but her matchmaking was a little weird. Then she told me everything. Every piece of food she doesn't sell to eat in the store is a human turned into some form of sweet to find love. When people enter the shop, they'll be instantly drawn to their soulmate and buy them. If they do the right thing and don't eat them, they'll end up falling in love with their match-made treat, and once the admission of love occurs, the spell is broken, and the person can become two things: a sweet treat and a human at their own will. A lot of people like sex with their treats, so that's why she does it. Weird, I know—"

"The best sex I've ever had in my life has been with a banana split. Weird is relative."

"Anyway, I instantly felt our connection when you picked my flavor. Our souls were meant to be. I fell madly in love with you at first sight and had to have you that night. I snuck into your room and made you mine."

I blush, thinking of the first night.

"Anyway, when you broke the spell and told me you hated sweets, I became a normal human again and couldn't turn into a sweet. My heart was broken. But then Mrs. Owens contacted me and told me that you came to her, begging me to come back and that you love me. She is a hopeless romantic and told me I had one shot. I could become the ice cream and human man again because our love was meant to be. So, that's what happened. But when I met you as a human, I had the urge to make you fall in love with the human me, too. But when I got here and saw how hot you looked, I wanted nothing more than to stick my banana in you. Let's say banana split sex is the best sex I've ever had and better than normal human sex. So, I couldn't help it. I shifted into my banana split form, and now... Here we are."

I don't know what to think. I don't know what to say. I should be mad at him for lying to me, making me unintentionally feel guilty about being in love with him and Rocky simultaneously, but he's both the ice cream and the man. And I know I can't let him go.

"Are you sorry you lied?" I ask.

He nods his head fervently. "Yes, so sorry. I feel so bad that I didn't tell you who I was and reveal myself immediately."

"Then I forgive you."

"Really?"

"Yes," I add. "Now," I grab him by the hair, "Turn this hair into hot fudge, and let's have the best ice cream sex in the world."

His eyes widen, and then his mouth morphs into a smile. "You got it, baby. But, do me a favor."

"Anything," I panted as his body shifted into an

ice-cold sundae before his fingers turned back into cones.

"Call me Alex, not Rocky."

I smile and pull his sprinkled lips to mine. "You got it."

Then he kisses me, his stickiness coating my lips as I lick into his ice-cold mouth. His body is on mine, making a complete melting mess, as he nudges my legs apart with his literal creamy thigh. He moves his hand down to my pussy and twirls rough waffle-coned fingers around my clit, giving me the exact pressure and texture I need. I'm panting and moaning as he uses his thick coned thumb to continue his ministrations and thrusts a wide cone into my pussy. It expands, and I cry out.

"That's right, baby, crumble my cone. Let my cream cover your insides."

I come around him with just his words; before I know it, he pulls out his cone and replaces it with his engorged banana.

Our eyes meet, mine and his gumdrop ones, and he says, "I'm going to split you so good with my banana."

"Fuck, yes!" I shout as he thrusts his banana into me and starts moving. He uses his hands to mold my breasts as I clench myself around his length. Fuck, his banana is so firm and thick. I've never had a banana this wide before.

"Merry Christmas, baby." He pulls out abruptly, and I gasp as he flips me onto my stomach and thrusts back in. He slaps my ass with his ice-cold palm, his fingers leaving indents all over my skin.

He pounds into me harder. "Come around, my banana, baby. I want to feel you clench me and cut my banana in half with just your pussy."

I cry out as I convulse around him, and he grinds his hips harder into me. He growls before he pulls out and shoots what smells like strawberry syrup all over my back.

"Fuck, fuck," He cries out.

I'm so spent and covered in his cream, chocolate, and syrup that I can barely breathe. I feel like I'm crashing from a sugar rush.

"You are so fucking hot," he falls onto the bed beside me. He shifts back into his human form, and I smile as I look at my ice-cream human man. "Sorry, I know you probably want to cuddle the ice cream, but I want to feel you, skin to skin, and warm you up. You're so chilly."

"Baby, It's Cold Outside," I smirk.

"Getting into the Christmas spirit now?"

"All I want for Christmas is you, Alex. That's all I want. And your ice cream."

He laughs and says, "All I want is you too, baby. You too. Merry Christmas."

epilogue

· · ·

*I*t's been three years now, and it's our wedding day. Alex and I have had the best relationship I could ever dream of. My life is a dream, and I am so happy. I never thought I could be like this. When I was with Duncan, things were never this good. We'd been together for years, but still, he was never this open, sweet, and sexy.

Alex has brought me so much joy over the years, in the bedroom and out, and finally, we're making it official.

Soon after he admitted who he was, I moved into his house in the Valley. I used the money I had from work that wasn't going to rent to go to culinary school and become a baker.

Shockingly, I went to Mrs. Owens's bakery again, and she offered me a job. I'm now the head baker at Matchmaker Baker, where we set up couples and bring people joy.

Libby, Krissy, and Jason are all my bridesmaids, and they're chatting, giggling about their lives, catching up with each other while I stand in front of the mirror and dream about the life Alex and I will have together.

Today is Christmas. It's like the wedding he spoke of to my mom. A Christmas wedding in a winter wonderland in New York, where we've never spent much time. It's a beautiful hotel where you can see snow falling, and everyone wants to warm up with a cup of hot cocoa. With marriage comes the potential for babies, and that sends my nerves into overdrive. I touch my stomach, thinking that I can get pregnant so soon now that I've stopped my birth control, as we discussed. I cringe when Krissy comes over and remove my hand from my belly.

"Are you ready, sis?"

"Yes," I say.

Dad walks into my hotel room with Mom at his side, dabbing happy tears with a handkerchief.

I take my dad's arm, and we walk to the gazebo in the most beautiful hotel I've ever seen. It's cold, my dress has long sleeves, and everyone is wearing winter coats. I don't know why we decided to do it outside, but Alex said he wanted the chilly weather to consume us the moment we say I do. Music plays as Dad walks me toward Alex, who looks the happiest any ice cream man/human could be. Ice cream. My body pulses with need just thinking about tonight and what fun will come. I have a big surprise for Alex. He wanted to try something but didn't think it was possible. Only he doesn't know that it is and that with Mrs. Owens's help, I'll make my banana split's dreams come true.

I get to the archway, and the minister says his peace. We say our vows, and before I know it, Alex is dipping me and kissing me so hard that I can feel his lips morph briefly into sprinkles.

The crowd claps, and we walk back down the aisle hand in hand. He twirls me around, and that's it. We're married.

*A*fter we've had the best time celebrating our marriage with our friends and family, I push Alex into our hotel room and say, "I have a surprise for you."

He morphs into his ice cream form. "Oh really, now?"

I bite my lip and close my eyes. My mind drifts to precisely what I want to become, and Alex gasps. "Oh fuck, me. You're good enough to eat."

I open my eyes and look down at my ice cream body. Alex told me he wanted to see what it would be like if we were both ice cream and molded together to become one big banana split, only I became a sundae.

I have cherries for nipples and a little cherry for a clit. My gumdrop eyes are green, unlike Alex's blue, and my ice cream color is a mix of peppermint ice cream mixed with candy cane pieces. My fingers are made of candy canes, and I smirk when I think of how tight they can morph together to grab his banana.

"You are so beautiful, I can't even believe I'm so lucky," Alex sounds so happy that it makes me feel the same.

I smile and glance in the mirror that's next to the door. I do look good enough to eat. I'm a Peppermint Christmas Sundae with caramel drizzle for my blonde hair.

"Are you ready to make a little scope of ice cream?"

His sprinkly smile widens, and he says, "Definitely."

He pulls me down to him, and our ice cream mixes together as we become one big sundae.

The End

art, art, art

Turn to page for some very special spicy artwork of scenes from the book!

bonus epilogue

. . .

5 years later

Alex

This year, I'm determined to make Katie the best Christmas ever. She's had it tough. The Matchmaker Bakery has been booming, and everyone has been raving about how you meet your soulmate there. She says she wishes she could tell people exactly how, but she doesn't. It's always a big surprise and a big secret, probably because people are ashamed.

I'm not ashamed in the slightest. I love our beginning, but I love how our life is going.

I'm just unloading the tree from my SUV when my two little sundaes run up and grab my legs.

"Whoa!" I gasp and nearly fall.

Katie's laughter from the doorway to our holiday

retreat makes my heart pound louder. She's beautiful and intelligent, and I love everything about this woman. She's the best thing that's ever happened to me. And these two little frosty sundaes are, too.

No, our twins are not ice cream. When Katie found out she was pregnant, she was scared that all they'd see on her ultrasound was a carton of Dryers. But the shock of shocks, our babies were all human and can't shift at all. Katie had to stay in her human form for her whole pregnancy, and once those six weeks were up afterward, she turned into the most delicious peppermint ice cream you'd ever taste.

Our little ones have no idea about mommy and daddy's unique abilities, though. They're only two wildlings. Riley is the more reserved one, always looking serious and stubborn. Meanwhile, Taylor is all sass, and I swear this toddler rolled her eyes at me the other day and flipped her hair. She's like her Uncle Jason, and sometimes it drives Katie nuts.

"Babies, if you hold daddy's pants like that, he's going to fall, and we won't be able to set up the tree."

"We'll set up this tree alright, but first..." I grab one and the other and pull my kids into my arms. I kiss their flushed little cheeks and pink noses. Their skin is so fair that it's easy to tell when they're cold. Taylor has blue eyes and dark hair like me, and Riley has green eyes and is blonde like Katie. I'm pretty sure my family is the best there ever was.

Katie smiles brightly at me and holds her arms out for me to enter the house.

I run with the twins toward the house, and they both giggle. Once inside, I hear Mariah Carey's "All I Want For Christmas." The air is warm and smells of honey ham and yams. The only thing we had left to do was get a tree, and though Katie had wanted to go two days ago, I insisted that I go alone today so we could spend time together as a family hiking and playing by the lake before it snowed. And boy, did it snow.

I place the kids on the couch and then turn to my wife.

"I have to bring that tree in here."

"I know," she says. Her hands are behind her back, and she's wearing a fuzzy green sweater and tight jeans that make her ass look great.

"You should have done this days ago. Now it's Christmas Eve, and it's nearly four in the afternoon."

"Watching them learn to set up the tree will be fun."

"Fun!" They shouted together, and Katie rolls her eyes.

"Bring in the tree, Rocky."

I smirk and leave the house without another word.

The night is still young by the time the twins fall asleep, and the tree is all lit up. Tomorrow, Katie's family and my parents are coming over, and we're going to have quite the time. Her mother loves touching my bicep, and her father only wants to watch old Christmas movies and then rant about the shitty lives the actors had.

Meanwhile, my parents are determined to do anything but play nice with my in-laws. They're determined to be the favorite grandparents and give the best gifts. The only problem is they don't even bother trying to spend time with the kids when they're around. That means that Katie's parents win the Best Grandparents Award.

We're cuddled on the couch, watching Home Alone and making out like teenagers.

I pull away from Katie and whisper, "You taste like cherries."

"You taste like hot fudge, but I want your banana."

"You want my banana... Here?"

She nibbles on her lip. "Well, we were talking about having another, right?"

"Yes," I say slowly. We've been trying for a while, then stopped, and have been talking again about trying for another baby, but it just hasn't happened for us.

"What if it's because we've been doing it wrong? What if I need your... banana to do the job."

"That makes no sense."

"We make no sense, dear. We're shapeshifting ice cream."

"Baby," I laugh, but she pounces on me. Her skin shifts icy cold, and my own turns hard like ice. I pull her close, and our creamy goodness combines. I dip my coned fingers into her bare pussy. She feels cold but warm at the same time and so wet. I don't know if it's her or the ice cream.

She takes my cock in her candy-cane fingers and wraps her hand around it. You'd think candy canes would just be sticky, but mixed with ice cream, the roughness of her fingers and the wetness from the cream make me nearly come from her touch.

I flip her over onto her back, getting cream everywhere, and then kiss down her body. I take one of her cherry nipples into my mouth and twirl my popsicle tongue over it. She moans and thrusts her body upward. Before she can say or do anything, I hum a song an ice cream man's truck makes while I thrust hard into her core. She feels human almost on the inside, like she's trying hard to keep herself that way, and I think maybe it's because she thinks that will help make a baby. Perhaps I should turn my banana into a regular cock too. I don't, though. The banana feels so good when it thrusts into her human body. She clenches around me and cries out as I pound harder into her.

"Say it with me, baby," I say, looking her in the eye.

"I scream." she moans as I move my hand to her clit.

"You scream," I growl.

"We all scream." We say together.

"For ice cream!" She cries out, and I cover her mouth with my dripping hand as I come inside her, causing fudge to pour everywhere.

"I love you, Alex." She breathes.

"I love you too, baby."

We cuddle up, her back to my front, and become one big ice cream scoop.

When we wake the following day, thankfully, no one is up to see that we're still in ice cream form. We shift quickly and go about our day.

As the family comes, eats, and we all enjoy the company, I look around at my kids and Katie and can't believe my luck. If I didn't walk into the Matchmaker Baker, I'd never have this life.

"Would you like some ice cream, Alex?" My mother-in-law asks.

"Only the one that Katie made," I wink at my wife across the table.

My mother-in-law looks confused, but I don't care. The only ice cream I'll ever want is right before me, and she'll keep me full until the end of time.

sugar & spice

Is He Naughty or Nice?

prologue

. . .

$\mathcal{I}$ don't know what brought me to the store or
why the gingerbread man looks so tasty, but
I know I must have it the second I see it.

one

. . .

I wake up in the night to get a glass of water. Having a sexy dream about the fucking cookie is a lot to take in. A fucking gingerbread man? What the fuck is wrong with me? What's that even about? And it wasn't just the one time, we fucked twice. The second time, he wasn't even a cookie anymore but a ginger-haired man with tan freckled skin and vibrant green eyes. His voice was deep and Irish, and my heart skipped a beat just thinking about it.

I fill my cup with water and then look at the gingerbread man in the box. My eyes widen at the missing man and the broken lid. I mutter, "Motherfucker."

No doubt my brother Jared broke into my cookie man's box.

I need to find an apartment for that asshole. He's twenty-eight and still living with his older brother, rent-free. I would probably throw him out on the street if it weren't for our mother. But Mom begged me to take him in. He's her baby and is "just trying to make it in the acting world, and you know how hard that can be!" Fucking bullshit. The guy goes on one audition for one play and doesn't even get the role, and Mom thinks he's a starving artist. The guy is well-fed because I feed him breakfast, lunch, and dinner. He spends most of his day working out and mooching off me.

Jared and I used to get along just fine, but then I came out, and things got weird. He says shit like, "No Homo," when his friends come over, and even they're like, "Dude, it's not 2005."

I place my cup on the counter and start toward the kitchen door, only to hear a toilet flushing from my half-bath, and the fucking gingerbread man strolls out as the toilet water continues to run.

My mouth drops as I watch the cookie man scratch his rippling muscles outlined with icing. Yes, the gingerbread man has a ripped body. How did the baker design him like that? She made him so realistic. He's a fucking cookie! But jeez, he's a hot cookie.

"Oh," he says with his red icing mouth. His eyes are icing, a light green, and his nose is a gumdrop. He has dotted brown freckles all over his face and arms, and my mind drifts to the human I fucked in my dream. "I thought I heard you get up, but I wasn't sure."

"You're alive?" I'm so shocked I don't know how the words get out of my mouth... Or why they're almost suggestive.

He laughs like he's shy and scratches his stomach again, drawing my eyes to his perfect V. I shoot them back up to his face when he says in a sweet, sexy accent, "In a way."

"What does kind of mean?"

"Um..." he avoids my gaze and says, "So, do you always like to pull out and cum on a guy's back, or did you just think I needed more icing?"

I sputter, "That was—that was a dream!"

"It wasn't. You came into the kitchen practically half asleep, and I was getting out of my box to come and see you."

"Come and see me?"

"I wanted to look at you."

"While I was sleeping? A gingerbread man left his box and wanted to watch me sleep. I don't know whether to be flattered or creeped out."

He's silent for a moment, and we stare at each other before he says, "You don't seem as shocked as I expected. You're conversing with a gingerbread man and not having a complete meltdown."

"Do most men or women have complete melt-downs when you come out of your box?" I don't know why I feel a hint of jealousy, but I don't like the idea of anyone tasting a single crumb of my gingerbread man. *My* gingerbread man? Like I own him... I mean, I did buy him.

"No other person has opened my box." If he were a person, like that Irish god that I dreamt about, he'd blush like a strawberry. "So, you're not shocked?"

Relief overwhelms me before I fold my arms and shrug, going with it. "Anything is possible. That includes a gingerbread man coming to life. Mrs. Owens did seem like a witch. I've met some when I was growing up. My mom was totally into tarot and shit."

He smiles. "I'd love to hear more about you."

"Yeah, before that, you have some explaining, Ginny, boy."

"Ginny boy?"

"I'm calling you Ginny. That good with you?"

He smiles, and my breath hitches. How can a cookie be so beautiful? True art. Katie was right. That woman is a true artist.

"Yeah, that's good with me."

"Good, now explain. How are you a cookie? And where did you come from? Are you just brought to life, or did you come from a person, or are you a person turned into a cookie because you pissed her off? Is she a good witch or a bad bitch?"

"She's uh... Well, I can't say. I'm not supposed to say."

"I'm going to think the worst then," I look at my manicured nails. I'm extremely into self-care. I liked to get facials, massages, and my nails done once a week. My ex called it narcissistic, but I like looking good and feeling good. Being a lawyer can be stressful. My brother calls me a "femme," but I don't care. I like what I like, and anyone else can suck a fuck.

"Okay." He nibbles on his lip. His teeth are made

of what looks like stiff white icing. It makes me wonder if his mouth tastes like gingersnaps or just plain sugar.

"So, what? You wanted to watch me sleep, but somehow, we ended up fucking?"

"Yeah, uh, you kind of saw me and like seduced me."

"But I thought you were a human."

"I uh... You weren't supposed to do that." He cringes. "I'm a gingerbread man... And a... A human of sorts."

"Of sorts? So, like a shapeshifter? A human and a gingerbread man. Interesting. I love it. Are you a gingerbread man because you're a ginger or a ginger because you're a gingerbread man? Wait, is everything ginger, including your pubes? Is that too much to ask? Jeez, sorry, I'm rambling." I laugh awkwardly.

He doesn't seem fazed by my response; he is only surprised. "Wait, you're okay with this?"

"Have you seen what the online dating scene looks like? A giant, talking cookie wouldn't even break the top 10 weirdest profiles I've swiped right on," I shrug thinking back to my dream and how I made a mess all over his marshmallow back. He's a gingerbread man that has rock-solid crispy cookie abs made apparent by stiff frosting and a soft squishy butt. And his cock... I vaguely recall it being like one of those cylinder cookies that's gingerbread flavored with a rounded tip and that it's not scratchy or anything but soft in my hand. And when he comes, he comes sugary icing and shudders so hard that some crumbs fall from him. I lick my lips thinking about it.

"Yes. I am a go-with-it guy, and you're a very hot gingerbread man. And I'm going to eat you up." I lick my lips.

two

. . .

We fuck again, and I have the best, softest asshole in my life. His doughy hole molds over my cock, and tightens around it, and it feels so fucking good.

One of the many times I vowed to myself, I don't know if I'll ever get enough of his marshmallow ass, and yet, at the same time, I know food expires at some point. I try not to think about it as we lie on our sides, facing each other on my filthy bed. It looks like I built and ate a whole gingerbread house with crumbs and icing. Even some marshmallow fluff around. I didn't know he could come both icing and marshmallow, but it just depends on how deep I get and how much he gets off on my touch.

His touch is soft as he rubs my arm up and down, and I don't know why his smooth, warm touch gets to me. As he does it, he feels like a cookie just out of the oven... He also tastes like one too. His insides are warm and gooey like he's not fully baked in there, but he's also firm and tight, which made me come so hard I almost blacked out.

"So, you're like a real baked good? Were you ever human?"

"Well... I'm human in a sense, as I said."

"Shapeshifter?"

"Not exactly."

"Is it like an essence? Like your soul or something?"

He frowns like he hates not telling me what's going on. "I can't say."

"Why is the witch giving pastries souls but also making them sign NDAs?" I snort, trying to make light of it. "Or you just won't tell me everything?"

"I... I can't." He pins me down to the bed and growls, "Now shut up. I want to give you an early Christmas Present."

"Well, Hanukah is coming up," I say. "And I am half Jewish. Call this one of eight gifts you need to— Oh Fuck—"

He kisses down my body, leaving a trail of icing before he gets to my cock and sucks it into his mouth. It feels like gooey heaven. I can't breathe or think as his soft, warm, spicy tongue licks me from the head to the base and then back again. He's so sweet and has a hint of chocolate to him. His mouth molds over my dick and tightens as it goes up and down. I lean back on my bed and grab his hair, saying, "Yes. Fuck yes. Fuck me with your mouth."

He continues to suck me off, and I moan as I can't control myself as I come down his throat. I don't know exactly where it goes, but this cookie doesn't have a gag reflex.

He pulls away from me, and we both breathe hard. His cookie shapeshifts out of focus briefly, and for a short moment, I see a human man with gingery red hair and freckles everywhere. He's back to a cookie before I can say or do anything.

"What's your name?" I ask softly.

"Ginny."

"I want to know your human name."

"I'm not supposed to—"

"Just tell me." I roll my eyes.

"Seamus O'Keefe."

I smile. "Okay, that's not a gingerbread man's name. I'm going to call you Ginny." I tease.

He laughs. "Sounds good."

"I like your name, though, very Irish. I'm wondering why an Irish man takes the shape of a gingerbread man, not some Irish Coffee-flavored thing."

He smiles his icing smile and says, "Whatever you say."

"What do you do for a living, *Ginny*?"

"I'm a gingerbread cookie at your service."

I shake my head. If he doesn't tell me anything tangible, I will go crazy. I want to know him more than just as a cookie. I never felt a connection with someone so much sexually or anything that would make me

want to learn more. Not even my previous relation-
ships made me want to know more about the guys.
They were primarily sexual and shallow. But there's
something about Ginny—Seamus that makes me want
to learn more. Call it fate or something, if possible, to
be fated to enjoy a cookie as more than just something
to eat.

"No, I mean as a human. You have to have a job if
you're a shapeshifter or something. Or if you were
cursed into this—"

"I—"

"I know you can't tell me, even if I'm dying to know
the truth. But give me something. I want to know more
about your favorite, about you. What do you like to
watch? What kind of books do you read? What's your
favorite cookie?" I nudge him, and he licks his lips with
his licking tongue, then sighs.

"I'm not supposed to tell you all of this. I could
turn into a crumbled cookie."

My eyes widen. "Are you serious?"

He snorts. "No. I can tell you a bit. I was a real
estate agent. Well, I own the agency."

I narrow my eyes at him. "Your human form looked
familiar."

He shrugs. "Ever look for a place to buy? I have
advertisements all over the city. Not that you probably
have seen them."

"Hmm," I try to think about it, but the only time I
went searching for a house other than my own years
ago was when I went to look at apartments for my

brother, but I didn't have a real estate agent with me or even look for one. We just went on our own. "So, are you Irish, or do you just use this accent to get guys into bed?"

"I'm from Dublin. I moved to America in my teens, and the accent never disappeared."

"How old are you now?"

"How old are you?" He counters. "If you want to know about me, I should know about you. It's only fair."

"True," I nibble on my lip. "I'm old."

"How old?"

"Thirty."

He barks a laugh.

"What's so funny?"

"I'm nearing forty in my human form."

"Forty and single. You make me look like a young spring chicken." I tease.

His smile vanishes, and he looks down. "I, uh, wasn't always single."

"Oh?" He looks so sad that I wonder if he's fresh off a breakup and the cookie thing was some curse because of an ex or something.

"I was married to a woman. We never had kids or anything, but I divorced her when I finally came out."

My heart races. I've never really dated women before or dated anyone who has. But married? "Was it... Recent?"

"About a year ago. Coming out was hard. I lost a lot of family and friends. My parents don't talk to me; I only ever speak to my little sister, Sally. She's about thirty, too. She said she always knew and was shocked I lasted this long without coming out."

"Well, at least you have a supportive family member. My mom is supportive, but my brother puts up with me and my dad... Well, he doesn't talk to me anymore."

"That's tough. I had a great relationship with my mum, but she always wanted grandkids and was more upset that she'd never get them. Like a gay man can't have kids. My dad, on the other hand, doesn't think the 'gay' thing will last and that I'm going through a phase but won't talk to me until it's over."

"That's tough."

"Yeah, I was close to them... Anyway," he looks over my shoulder at the time. "It's getting late, and you should go back to bed before you wake up for work."

"True..." I say, and then I pounce. I kiss him hard and bite his gingerbread lip enough to tear off a piece. My eyes grow wide, and I pull back. I can't help but chew.

"It's okay," he says as the cookie regenerates, and I gape at him. "I'm made for your pleasure in all ways."

I laugh, and then we start talking more about our favorite things. It's not long, though, before I begin to drift to sleep. I dream of months ago when I was looking for an apartment for my brother, and some real estate guy brought someone else to see the apartment. He watched me with intent and had a hot Irish accent. I couldn't help but want to ask him for his number, but my brother caused a scene, and then I never saw the guy again. I know it must have been Seamus, but maybe he doesn't remember me.

As I sleep, I hear Ginny say, "Dreams do come true. I've loved you since I met you months ago. I hoped that you would come into the store and find me. And when you did, I was so happy that you bought me. It was fate—destiny. But I can't imagine a person like you loving someone like me. I'm just a barely out gay with low self-esteem. You practically exude confidence, and I'm just trying to get mine back and embrace my identity. I'm a divorced guy who hid in the closet for years. But I can accept myself a little more if I have you. All I can think about is that you'll say the words I'm terrified of. Not the words I want to hear most. I love you, Jason. I wish you'd love me back."

I want to tell him with a body and personality like his, he's got nothing to worry about confidence-wise. I lost friends and family members when I came out, too. I've only started to embrace who I am over the last few years. I continue to sleep and don't respond. It has to be a dream, after all. He says he loves me and doesn't believe I can love him back. It might be fast and almost instant, but after everything I've learned about him and everything we've done tonight, I can't let Ginny— Seamus go. If there were ever a case of instant fated love, it would be what I feel for this gingerbread man.

My heart speeds up, but I cuddle into his warm, cookie body and sleep.

three

. . .

Five hours later, I've been overwhelmed with cases and calls. I'm putting out fires for my clients left and right. I now know that taking an afternoon off is not possible. I may stop work at 5 pm and go home, but that's when most decide they are too tired to bother with their cases, so I get a break. But if I leave in the afternoon, I will have so much work to catch up on the next day. Fuck I love and hate my job so much. I love the thrill of the courtroom and helping my clients. I'm a personal injury and civil litigation attorney. But the paperwork and dealing with every-thing that goes into my job, discovery, pleadings, it's all so... tiring sometimes.

I always go into the office early, and Ginny, my gingerbread boyfriend, was curious, so I brought him along. I asked him first, of course, and he was all for it. Then we fucked again before we left my room. His doughy hole molded over my cock, and tightened around it, and it felt so fucking good.

I packed him up, and we made our way to my office.

Now I'm exhausted and need a freaking break after the phone call with my client. I slam my phone down and sigh. I scrub my face as I review another case file, but it's all gibberish. I push away from my desk and say, "I really shouldn't do this at work, but..."

I open my drawer and pull Ginny out of his box.

"Ginny, you can come out now."

"I don't know, last time I did that, it didn't end well," he replies.

I watch as the gingerbread man becomes human-sized, though he's not human at all. Then, before he says anything, my eyes narrow in on his face; it's so human yet still so cookie-like. I push him up against my desk and devour his mouth with mine. He tastes like nutmeg and Christmas, and I want to consume every inch of him. He moans as I chew on the piece of cookie from his lip. Then I flip him around and bend him over my desk. Icing smears all over my paperwork, but I don't care. I want nothing more than to sink into him.

"What do they say, you gingerbread men say, 'run, run, as fast as you can, you can't catch me. I'm the gingerbread man?' Well, I caught you, Ginny. And I'm going to eat you up."

"Eat your heart out, Jase," he says breathlessly.

I love that he calls me that. His deep Irish tone makes it sound husky and sexy, and it makes me bite into his neck. I take a piece of cookie off of him and chew his yummy goodness as he moans. It's getting weird doing that, but he seems to like it.

I undo my belt buckle and then pull my pants down just below my erect cock. I spread his soft marshmallow cheeks apart and say, "I'm going to thrust into your warm gooey asshole and see if we can't make a gingerbread man cream-filled."

"You're so weird," he chuckles, but I thrust into him, and he groans.

I don't need lubricant because it's so soft and gooey on the inside. I slap his marshmallow ass that jiggles before I pound harder into him. "Fuck, you're the best Christmas gift I've ever had. I love sweets, and your ass is the sweetest."

"Shut up and fuck me, Jase."

"Oh, I'll fuck you alright. I'll make sure you shoot icing all over this fucking room. I don't care if I have to have the janitor in here and tell them I had a cookie decorating party."

I fuck him hard and fast, grinding my pelvis against his ass with every thrust. I move my hand to his cookie cock and jack him off.

I'm so overwhelmed by the sensation I can't control myself before I come into him, messing up his insides and letting his warm center squeeze around me.

He's moaning but hasn't come yet.

"Fuck, fuck." I mutter before I pull myself out. I let go of his cock and then get to my knees before flipping his body around.

"You don't have to—"

"I want to," my voice is rough, and I'm breathing hard. I bend down and take his cookie cock in my mouth. He tastes like liquid sugar and spices. His precum tastes like spiced custard from eggnog, and I lap it up as I take him to the back of my throat. He grabs my hair in his hand. His fingers are soft and leave crumbs in my gelled hair. He tugs my head back, and I look into his drawn eyes before he says, "I'm going to make you so full you'll never want to eat another sweet again."

He pulls out of me briefly, and I breathe, "Promise?"

He thrusts into my mouth, and I gag around him, nearly biting him, but I refrain from doing it.

I lick him from top to bottom and down to his gumdrop balls. I take one into my mouth and suck on it. He shivers.

"Fuck, that's good."

I pull back and lick up his shaft before he retakes control, tangling his fingers in my hair and slamming harder and faster into my mouth.

"I'm coming," He grunts, and his accent is so sexy and thick it makes me think of Irish Crème. "I don't want you to choke on my icing."

He pulls my head back even though I want just that and then turns his body and comes all over my floor. Pieces of crumbs litter my floor, and a big dollop of icing soaks into my rug.

My eyes stay on the carpet before he says, "That was," he's breathless.

I look into his eyes and say what I know he wants to hear and what I want to tell him more than anything, "I don't think I can live without you, Ginny—I mean Seamus. I love you as a gingerbread man and want to get to know you as a human. This was hot, but I want to fuck the real you. I think I'm falling in love with you. No. I'm in love with you."

His eyes widen.

There's a knock on my office door, and I jump up. "I'll be right back," I say. I pull my pants up and wipe my mouth with my shirt sleeve. I grab my jacket and put it on so no one will see. Ginny is standing there, still in shock. My hands are shaky, and my breath is ragged. My mind is consumed with racing thoughts.

Isn't that what he wants to hear? It's what I want to say, but from his stunned reaction—maybe I'm a fool.

I turn from him and go to the door, where I find Merial, Duncan's secretary. I make sure she can't see in my office. She's so frazzled she doesn't seem to care to try to look. "He's harassing her. You might want to help Katie."

I nod. It's a code red for our friend group.

"I'll be right back." I don't bother to look at my gingerbread lover again; I'm too nervous to.

Then I leave the office and go to save my friend.
***

When Libby and Katie leave my office, I nibble on my lip and go to my desk drawer, where I figured

Seamus—not Ginny—Seamus went back to. But when I look, he and the box are gone.

My heart races, and I feel like I can't breathe. I look around my office for my missing gingerbread boyfriend and panic. Did he go outside the office? Did he reveal himself? Did he change back into his human form and leave me?

That last thought makes my heart feel like a burnt cookie cracking in half.

I told a gingerbread man-shifter I love him, and he disappears!

Tears prick my eyes, and then Libby intercoms me. "Jason... I want to know more about the gingerbread man."

I sniffle and pick up the phone. I clear my throat, pretending that I'm sick. "Sorry, Libs, my throat aches from sucking his magic cookie cock. Talk to you later."

"Jase—"

I hang up the phone and do some breathing techniques to calm my breaking heart.

This is why I never date. This is why I never reveal my feelings. I'm an asshole. Everyone knows it. I'm sassy and fabulous but an asshole. I don't take shit from anyone. I protect my friends at all costs, and right now, I will be there for Katie.

I straighten my tie and get up from my desk. I notice the icing and crumbs on the carpet of my office, and as I walk past and exit my office, I call out in the nastiest tone I can make, "Someone was eating a cookie in my office today. Who was it?"

Everyone around stops and looks at each other. I shake my head and say, "Get your shit together, guys. This is a law firm, not a fucking bakery."

I head back into my office and call the janitorial service before bawling my eyes out.

christmas eve

. . .

It's been weeks since I last saw Ginny, AKA Seamus. My heart still aches, but I decide to take action and not let people walk all over me anymore. I tell the partners to get their shit together with Duncan and Arabella threatening them and causing trauma for my best friend. I tell them that if they're so scared of their wives because they cheated on them with the office ho, they shouldn't have fucked someone else, and I say to them that Arabella is known for trying to sleep her way to the top or brag about it and say that they should say she threatened them about it. I'll back them up on that and on Duncan being a blackmailer. I tell them I'll file the restraining order and call HR to fire both of them.

They like that I'm so strategic about it; they agree to give Katie her regular position back, and Arabella and Duncan's offices are cleared out overnight.

I've spent my time working my ass off and finding my brother an apartment. I tell my mom I'm done taking care of him. He's an adult, and if he can't make it alone, he's a loser. She's disappointed in me, but I hear my father in the background saying, "Good!" Then he gets on the phone, shockingly asks how I'm doing, and says he's proud I'm growing a backbone. We don't talk about my sexuality, but he does say he'll see me for New Year's dinner and adds, "If you, uh, have someone you want to bring, uh, you can." It's awkward, but my heart is a cookie whose dough rises and becomes an edible, delicious baked good.

My brother shocks me by telling me he wants to prove himself and is tired of being the family loser. He moves out within a week. Initially, I'm relieved, but then loneliness sets in, and most nights, I sit at home, eating carrot sticks while I watch Hallmark movies with the same plot, just different actors playing characters with other names. I cried a few times, wishing someone would love me like that.

I've been masturbating to dreams of my ginger-bread man. Sometimes, he's in human form; at other times, he's a cookie. I'm not sure what you're supposed to feel when you walk past the baking aisle of the supermarket, but mournful and horny probably isn't the right response.

Sometimes, after work, I get a drink and try to take a guy home, but I always kick them out when they touch me.

Today is Christmas Eve, and I'm at home, eating

dinner by myself that I order from some fancy restaurant I had never heard of but pretend to be dying to eat at in front of my friends. The food is all pretty, but the portions are tiny.

My mind wanders to Ginny/Seamus and how I wish I could see and feel him, not just his gingerbread self but the human. I barely know the guy, but I don't want our connection to crumble away. Maybe it's because it's the holiday season and I'm lonely. Libby goes to see her family, and Katie is having dinner with her boyfriend, some human guy she met who looked like her banana split man, but apparently, she thinks that the wicked witch just stole the guy's essence to make the ice cream hunk.

I have a bottle of wine open; my large wine glass is empty, and my stomach is full of all the sweets and goodies people gave me for the holidays. Though I can't think about eating them without thinking about Ginny, I can't help it. I want something sweet and something to remind me of him.

Just as another Hallmark movie starts on my television, there's a knock at my front door.

I groan, not wanting to get up. I'm not drunk, but I just don't want to see or deal with anyone right now. I teased Katie about being a bah-humbug earlier this month, but lately, I've been super cranky at the office.

I didn't tell my friends what happened with Ginny. They still think that he's with me. Katie was heartbroken when she said, "I hate sugar," and Rocky disappeared. But I didn't do that. I told my gingerbread boyfriend that I loved him. Maybe next time, I should get an Oreo or something instead of something with spices. Oreos still have icing, but the chocolate is comfort.

I go to my door, but my doorbell keeps being bashed. Someone wants my attention, and I feel it's my brother.

I answer the door and say, "Dude, stop, I told you go to Mom's for Christ—"

"I'm sorry," An Irish accent I thought I'd never hear again says. My eyes widen as they take in Ginny—I mean Seamus.

"Ginny?"

He smiles shyly at me. Seamus has lightly tan skin with freckles everywhere. He has red gingery hair and a beard I didn't expect him to have. He's like a hot ginger Santa in a business suit. He has some laugh lines, and his body is like a hot bodybuilder, and the urge to ravage him consumes me even though I want to slap him. He smells like fucking sugar and spice, but I'm not sure if he's naughty or nice. After everything he's put me through, I want to give him a lump of coal, and yet, at the same time, I want to have this Ginger Santa become a cookie so I can milk him.

"I wanted to come sooner, but I was nervous." He sounds nervous. That's for sure. But even though I'm in a lust-filled haze and my heart races, he shattered it, and I don't know what to do.

"Nervous?" I test out the words, and then after, I

shout, "Nervous! I told you I am in fucking with love you, and then you disappear!"

He frowns and looks around to see if anyone can hear us outside.

I roll my eyes. "Don't worry, my neighbors know I have a hectic love life. They've been whispering about all the guys leaving here lately."

I have to dig at him, but it doesn't have the same outcome I want. His face does fall, and he looks hurt, but he doesn't yell or shout back at me. Instead, he says, "I... I just... Can I come in?"

I should turn him away, but I don't. I open the door wider for him to enter, and he walks through the doorway and toward my kitchen like he's on a mission. I roll my eyes, but even though I'm trying hard to be tough, my heart is beating a mile a minute, and I want nothing more than to tackle him. What can I say? I'm horny, and I'm also still madly and hopelessly in love with this man, even though we only spent a night and half a day together. How can I be so in love with him? I don't know, maybe it's fate, but why would he disappear on me if it is?

I follow him into the kitchen and find him taking a wine glass that matches my empty one and pouring my wine into his cup.

"What are you doing?"

He stops pouring into his glass halfway and pours the same amount into my cup. He doesn't even answer me, and it's getting on my nerves, but a part of me is so happy to have him in my space again that I don't want to scare him away. God, I'm suck a sucker for this cookie, man.

He pisses me off. Maybe being told I love him is too fast for him. It's an instant-love situation, and I've always thought that concept is stupid.

He sighs. "Maybe we should sit down, have some wine and talk. It's a long story, and I want you to be comfortable with it."

"You poured the wine already. Made yourself at home." I hiss, then say, "You want me to be drunk for this conversation, and then what? Will you take advantage of me?"

The thought makes my cock twitch. *Down boy.*

"No!" His face turns ashen. "I just know you like wine, and it calms you even when you don't have much. Not that you're a lightweight or anything."

"How do you know so much about me? You were stalking me, huh?"

"I wasn't stalking you. I mean, I liked you the moment I saw you when I was showing that apartment to my client. But I didn't stalk you or anything. I didn't know your name; you just stuck in my head. But after I was a cookie and you told me you loved me, I wanted to watch you get to know you, but I was scared to show my human side. You loved the gingerbread man, but the human? And the sex? Would you enjoy sex with a human when you don't think it's a dream? Or would you only ever want the cookie me? I loved you at first sight, but I knew it was stupid. Then we met like this, and you said you loved me too. I got scared, and when I turned back into a person—"

"Turned back into a person."

"The baker, Mrs. Owens, does this thing where you become a baked good at night or whenever you want to become one for the person you are with... When they aren't around, you're human again, but you can't approach the person. I didn't even get a chance to get back to human form before you said the magic words. Well, except for when we fucked that one time."

"So, you were human!"

"I wasn't supposed to be. I only was supposed to be a baked good with you. But the connection between us was so much, and I loved you so much that I think the spell was breaking, and the magic words weren't needed completely because how I felt for you was so strong."

"Magic words?"

"The spell breaks when your lover says, 'I love you' or something along those lines. Then you are bonded to that person, like a soulmate. You then can shift between forms easily if you want, and you don't just stay baked good in the person's presence. If you say anything like you don't love them or hate sugar, then the baked good becomes a person and will never turn into a baked good again. They'll have to move on. But I love you so much, and you love me, and my spell was broken, and now... I mean, if you want, we're meant to be. We're bonded, but I was scared."

I want to jump for joy, but I give him my resting bitch face because I don't want him to know just how excited that makes me.

"She's a crafty witch," he adds when I say nothing. "She can sense your soulmate when you enter her bakery looking for love. She lures your other half to the bakery, and boom, you guys are together. She had a pretty much a hundred percent satisfaction rate until a few weeks ago. She was pissed about it, but I'm hoping that changes."

"Katie," I say, thinking about my friend who didn't bring up her ice cream lover and is dating a human now.

"Yeah, anyway, I was scared that you only wanted me as a cookie and had to cope with just dealing with that. I had to consider whether I would always be a gingerbread man to you."

"That's stupid."

He frowns.

"You told me your name when we met. You told me you were human and turned into a baked good. You lied that you were a gingerbread man shapeshifter, though. That's what you are now."

He nods.

"I fell in love with *you*, the person and the cookie. It's not just the amazing marshmallow cookie sex, though it is the best sex I ever had." I feel my skin heat.

"Really?"

"Really. I love you, Seamus."

"I love you, too, Jason."

The next thing I know, he moves in on me. His lips mesh with mine, and our tongues are tangling before I can even think straight.

We're tearing at each other's clothing and moving to my bedroom.

He pushes me onto the bed and says, "I know that I just made a big deal about wanting you to love me as a person and not a cookie, but the sex was..."

"The best," I repeat.

"Yeah. Do you... Want me to?"

"It's up to you. I want you for you, Seamus, and if that's what you want to fuck me as, feel free."

He smiles, and the next thing I know, he's shifting into his cookie form, but his cock stays human. It's bigger than the cookie version, and the veins look tasty. It's half human and half cookie since his veins are outlined with icing. "I want you in my warm gooey marshmallow ass."

"You have no idea how much I want to be inside you," I growl as I pounce on him. I flip him onto his stomach and pull his ass upward. I slap it, watching it bounce and wanting to take a bite out of it. I unbutton my pants and pull them below my ass, and then before he can even say anything else, I thrust into him. He's tight and soft, and I slam into him over and over again. His warmth makes me nearly come right away, but I don't. I grab hold of his stiff more human cock and start jerking it. He groans as I fuck him nice and slow. It's soft and silky, and the icing turns into soft liquid sugar that spreads over him. I'll want to lick that off him after this.

"Faster," he breathes.

"If you insist," I smirk, and then I pound into him, letting his asshole tighten around my dick and stroking him faster. His sweet, spicy scent makes me bed down and bite into his neck. He cries out as he comes icing, and I can't hold back. I chew on his soft, spiced body and pound into him. "You're just sugar and spice and both naughty and nice! Fuck, I'm so glad I caught you, my gingerbread man."

"I'm not running anywhere." He pants.

Before I know it, I come so hard my vision blurs, and it's nearly hard to breathe. He collapses on my bed and instantly shifts into his human form. His asshole is tighter around my cock than him in his cookie form, but it's soaked from my cum. I moan, not wanting to leave him. I can feel myself growing hard while inside him.

"Fuck, I don't know what I like more," I whisper in his ear. "Your gooey center or your tight hole."

Then I start pounding into his human body, using my own cum as a lubricant, and he cries out, moaning as we go again.

We're at it all Christmas Eve, fucking, then taking a break for milk and, yes, cookies. He shifts between his cookie and human forms, and I realize just how much I love all of him.

As he drifts to sleep, I brush his hair out of his face and say, "I love you, Seamus."

"Ginny. Call me Ginny." He smiles warmly at me. "I love you too, Jase, more than anything."

"Merry Christmas." I press a kiss on his nose.

"Merry Christmas." He says.

And then we cuddle until the sun comes out and spend our first of many Christmas mornings together.

epilogue

. . .

"You look so delicious. Is this how you felt when you first fucked my marshmallow ass," Seamus grunts as he pounds his cock into my warm center.

After Katie's wedding, she told me the little surprise secret she had for her wedding night to her husband. So I returned to Mrs. Owens and asked for the same thing because tonight was the night I wanted to give Seamus the best gift.

"I, um," I can't think straight as he fucks into my ass.

Suddenly I'm coming and squirting out eggnog since I took the form of an eggnog cookie man with a marshmallow butt too.

I didn't want to look exactly like my gingerbread man. Being in gingerbread form is weird, but I'm still very much myself, just a crumbly cookie.

He slams his dick inside me one more time and comes, mixing his salty cum with my sweet core.

When he pulls out, we're both spent and breathing heavily.

"I love you," he says as he kisses my lips.

"I love you too." I hold my finger to him and say, "One sec."

I turn to my side table and open the drawer. I pull out a jewelry box and then turn back to him, only to find him holding a jewelry box as well.

My heart goes pitter-patter, and I feel so full of love and cum and just everything good and happy in the world.

It's Christmas time once again, and I never thought this could ever be my life.

"I see we have the same desires."

"Lots of them after tonight." I laugh. Pull him to me and kiss him.

He passionately kisses me before pulling away and saying, "I haven't said anything yet."

"Neither have I," I say. "But I'm ready to."

"I've been ready since the moment I met you."

We both open our ring boxes for each other, and I gasp at the beautiful gold engagement ring engraved with little gingerbread cookies. I look down at my ring that was probably just as expensive as his because it's the same.

We both laugh.

"That jeweler must have been very confused," I say.

"Look on the inside of yours." He says.

"You do the same." I'm shocked we both had the same idea.

I look at the engraving that says, "I ran, and you caught me. I plan to keep you for the rest of our lives."

Tears prick my eyes. He looks at his engraved one, and tears pour down his face.

"I know it's not as good as yours, but..."

"You want to grow old with me until we crumble in the wind," He speaks.

"Longer than that. We're not that old. Someone is going to figure out how to keep us alive forever. And if we have to be cookies that magic never makes stale, then it'll be worth it."

"I love you, Jason."

"I love you too, my Gingerbread man."

something special
for you

. . .

ginny

I walk into his room just as he's dozing, and he instantly sits up at the sight of me.

"What the fuck?" He bolts upright, and even though he looks sleepy, his eyes darken at seeing me.

"You look good enough to eat."

"Uh, I think I'm supposed to eat you. Tomorrow. Like the baker said." Jason says.

I laugh, and it comes out huskier than ever. He blushes, and I like the look on his face. I see the outline of his hard cock through his boxer briefs, and I lick my lips. I taste the icing, and I can't help but wonder if I'm a cannibal for wanting to lick my lips clean of the sweetness.

I end up saying, "That's exactly what I want."

Jason nibbles on his bottom lip, and I stalk toward

him. He watches me, not bothering to move. There's no fear in him like I thought there would be.

"You want me to eat you?" Jason asks.

"I want you to eat my marshmallow ass and then fuck it as hard as you can."

Jason swallows audibly, and I watch his Adam's apple bob before I make it to his side of the bed and kneel before him. He moves his legs off to the side of the mattress and spreads them, showing me just how excited he is. My cookie hands tug at his boxers and pull them down. His human cock is freed, and before he can do or say anything, I take it in my mouth.

Jason groans and says, "Fuck, your mouth is so warm and gooey. Damn."

I shove him to the back of my throat and swallow. My body is different than an average human's, and because I'm not hollow on the inside, my mouth and throat close around him, and he cries out and thrusts into me. I don't necessarily need to breathe in this form, and I have no gag reflex. As I take him so far down my throat, he pushes my cookie head all the way down on him. I lick him, and I can feel my icing coat on his cock.

Before I know it though, he pulls me back and pushes me away.

"Fuck," His forehead is beading with sweat as he looks me up and down. "Fuck, I was fucking a cookie's mouth."

"And you enjoyed it," I say. "Now, fuck me in the ass."

Jason hesitates for a moment, and I think maybe he won't before he grabs hold of my arms, crumbs littering the floor before he throws me face down onto the bed and slaps my marshmallow ass. I don't know why the baker decided to make my ass a marshmallow, but she thought it would be interesting, and it really is. It feels so good having his palm run up my ass until it teases my hole.

"Fuck, this ass is so squishy I can't wait to fuck it, eat it, I'm going to fuck you so hard, cookie man."

I snort, but then he grips my dick and tugs. A small amount of liquid icing drips out of me, and he scoops it up on his fingers and then moves it to my asshole. He teases my hole with his fingers before he slowly pushes it inside.

I moan, and he mutters another curse. "So tight, but so gooey and soft. You're half-baked in there."

"Yes," I pant as he shoves two fingers inside me and starts to stretch me.

This is a new sensation than it ever has been before. My cookie ass molds around his finger, and he hisses before he pulls them out and says, "I can't wait anymore. I'm going to cum if I don't fuck you right now."

"Then do it." I push my ass up for him, and he slaps it. I feel my cheek jiggle before he thrusts into me. I cry out, but not from pain. It might hurt if a guy didn't use any lube, but this is different. I am not fully baked in there, and my dough is raw.

He pounds into me, grabbing my ass and molding it,

then slapping it as he continues to thrust. I grab hold of my dick and start tugging on it. But I need him. I want him.

"Touch me," I beg.

"With pleasure." He says as he moves his hand to my cookie cock and starts tugging. "God damn, that feels so weird and yet good."

"Oh yeah," I groan as he continues to tug me and thrust at the same time.

Before I know it, he says, "I'm going to cum and fuck up your insides. You're going to be one salty cookie."

Then he tugs me faster, and thrusts become frenzied. He grunts as he comes and demands, "Come for me, gingerbread man."

With just his words, I do. I shoot icing all over his bed, and he says, "Jeez, you cum so much."

I'm so spent that I collapse on his bed, but that's not all. He says, "Just you coming makes me hard. I need to have you again."

And he does. He takes me harder this time, and I'm out of breath and can barely breathe when he pulls out and shoots his load all over my ass and back.

"I just ruined a cookie." He said. "No one said I was a good baker."

I laugh, and then he collapses on top of me.

I roll him off of me and then lay next to him as he falls fast asleep. I watch him for a while before I feel my body unintentionally shift into my human form.

Panic overcomes me as his eyes slowly open, and

he smiles drowsily. "You are a beautiful gingerbread man. Even as a fantasy in human form. I want to fuck you just like that."

Before I can do anything, like transform back into my gingerbread self, he rolls on top of me and pulls my legs around his waist. I don't know how he can go so much or get ready for it so fast, but he uses what was once icing and is now just my cum to wet my hole and teases it before he moves to thrust inside me. It feels good to be fucked like a human, but not as much as a gingerbread man. He moves slowly in me, and it's like he's making love to me. He kisses my lips, and I kiss him back.

"You still taste like a cookie." He slurs before he moves faster, and my orgasm starts to build. "Come with me, Ginny."

And I do. We both cum at the same time and then he finally collapses on top of me completely.

I pant and try to catch my breath. He's fast asleep. I can't sleep, though, and instead get up to go to the bathroom.

I run into his brother in the hallway, who rolls his eyes and says, "Seriously, you'd think he'd have the guys wear underwear while walking around."

He returns to his room, and I enter the bathroom and look myself in the mirror. I piss and clean myself up before I hear footsteps from outside. I feel he's up, and I use all my might to shift back into my cookie form. I know the rules, after all. Then I muster up all my courage and smile as I flush alerting him someone is here before I exit the bathroom.

He doesn't seem to remember most of what happened in the last few hours but thinks of it as a dream, and it breaks my heart a little. But at the same time, I'm not determined to make Jason mine.

a candyman for christmas

prologue

. . .

I didn't expect to find anyone I could love when I walked into the Matchmaker Baker's bakery. But the moment I saw my chocolate candy man, I knew I would love eating him up. Little did I know that he wasn't just something to eat when I wanted to binge and mope around. He was something entirely different...

one

. . .

"*D*ear fucking god," I moan as Pepper pounds his long and hard round-tipped candy cane dick into my pussy. I'm panting as he uses the curved digits of his candy cane fingers to wrap around and squeeze my nipple.

"That's a good girl, come for me. Come all over my peppermint cock."

"Fuck, fuck, fuck," I start to convulse around him as he moans. His thrusts grow frenzied. Fucking a peppermint candy bar is the weirdest thing I've ever done. I feel like this is something that people go to the hospital and get x-rays for, and the doctor says, *"Don't stick that up there! But oh my! How is that peppermint stick so big?"*

His chocolaty goodness covers my body, and he moves his thumb into my mouth. Chocolate drips into my mouth, and I twirl my tongue around him before he mutters, "Jeez, you're on the naughty list, aren't you?"

Then he starts pounding into me. "I'm going to make you come again, and if you don't, I'm giving you coal."

He moves his thumb from my mouth and toward my clit, and he starts rubbing. The melted chocolate gives his fingers extra moisture that's mixed with my cum. I've never squirted before, but as I come again, I do. It's all because he slams his candy cock into me, and his round-mint balls hit against my ass. My need for him to touch me *there* makes me cry out.

"You like when my mints slam into your ass? Do you want me in your asshole, baby?"

"Yes," I groan.

He pulls out of me, and I sob at the loss of him. Then he flips me over, and I gasp when he slaps his palm on my ass. It feels like little canes are hitting me. I should want to cry. I should be in pain, but I want him too much to feel anything else.

The next thing I know, I hear him spit on my asshole. I know it's gooey chocolate he's using as he coats me and then uses his fingers to stretch my hole. "You're so tight here. I can't wait to get my candy cane into this ass. I'm going to impale you so hard on my candy cock. You'll never want anything but minty goodness again. I bet it will tingle. You'll feel full and fresh."

"Stop talking and fuck my asshole and pussy with your canes," I growl.

"Are you my little ass slut? Not such a good girl, huh?" He's teasing me, and I can't take it anymore.

"I'm a very good girl, so fuck me," I push my ass

back, and then he shoves two fingers in and out of my hole. He laughs as I push against his fingers, needing him so badly.

"Fuck, this is going to feel so good. I want to feel you clench around me. I want you to break off a piece of my candy."

Then he flips me back onto my back, and my eyes widen. I look at his body, and it's a chocolate mold with candy cane pieces throughout him. And his cock. Well, *cocks,* plural, are staring at me, happy and erect. With one hard thrust, he enters my ass with one and my pussy with the other. I scream. It's not painful. It feels so good, and I feel so full. He moves his finger to my slit and teases my clit as he hammers his candy hard into me.

"Fuck, it's like both my dicks are rubbing together, and your pussy is squeezing one while your asshole... Fuck. I'm going to make you come so hard. You're so fucking hot. Do you like it when I thrust into both your holes? When you're so full, my sweetness?"

"Yes." I pant as he continues to fuck me.

He keeps at it, then does something I don't expect. He moves his candy cane finger into my mouth and tells me, "Suck." I do, letting the peppermint and sugar make my orgasm all the sweeter. I cry out and spasm around him.

"Shit! That's it. Come around, my candy, like the good girl you are. I can feel you milking me from your asshole."

I keep coming as he moves his fingers away from

my clit and out of my mouth. I'm gasping for breath as he grabs my hips and starts pounding into both my holes. But it's my ass that's bringing me back to life. My body might be spent, but I'm so consumed with a need I never thought I'd have before that I grind my body against him, meeting his thrust for thrust.

"Take my candy, baby. I'm going to fill you with my chocolaty seed."

His dirty words send me over the edge, and I come just from him being in my ass. He grunts and pulls out of me and shoots minty chocolate cum all over my belly with one cock, and the other shoots liquid peppermint. I feel like I've been dosed in peppermint hot chocolate.

Then he collapses on top of me, spreading his chocolate and peppermint cum on both of us.

"Was it good for you?" He says softly as he leans up on his elbows and looks me right in the eye.

"Fuck yes," I smile as I look into his white chocolate molded eyes that have brown irises.

He smiles, showing off his square mint teeth before he kisses my lips.

I kiss him back before he pulls away and says, "Do you like my peppermint kisses?"

"So much."

"And praise kink... Though you like being called a little ass slut didn't you?"

I feel myself blush.

He pulls away from me and flops onto the other side of my bed. I nibble on my lip and debate whether I should cuddle up to him. We've cuddled every night since I bought him, and he kisses my forehead before I drift off to sleep.

When I wake every morning, though, he's not here; he's fast asleep in his box. It makes my heart ache, thinking he might not want to sleep all night with me.

I'm so crazy. I'm questioning the feelings of a candy bar! What's worse is I've fallen in love with him!

He's shown me nothing but love and care when we talk, drink hot cocoa, and cuddle up to watch a movie. When we get to this stage of the night, he becomes a different candy bar. He goes from being sweet, giving me peppermint kisses, watching Hallmark movies, and making Die Hard Christmas jokes to being a dirty candy cane that makes a chocolate mess of me.

But all I want for Christmas is something I can never truly have. I want to keep him forever. But everything has an expiration date—even candy.

two

. . .

*I*t's been weeks, and I don't know how I can function with the amount of chocolaty good sex we've been having. I haven't had such great sex in, well, ever. I like to be sassy and talk big in front of my friends. But really, I'm just a thirty-year-old woman who's had two lovers before Pepper and never had an orgasm from someone other than myself before him. I've always wanted a family, and as my sisters and brothers married young and started families, I felt insufficient, though I'm more successful. I don't need Mom and Dad's money to help me, but it's still hard being alone most holidays when my whole big, happy family surrounds me.

If I could, I'd make Pepper an actual human, not a candy bar, though candy sex is fantastic. I still want that family and marriage. But how can I bring a piece of chocolate home to my family and say, "Hey, this is my boyfriend. He's a peppermint candy bar. He gives me the best orgasms, and he and I have a lot in common."

Yeah, no. First, I'm not going to tell my family about the orgasms, and second, they'll think I'm crazy or that the house is full of gas, and they're all going to die from a hallucination.

It's been weeks, and Christmas Eve is tonight. I told my family I had a date, and they were all excited for me, thoroughly understanding and then wondering how serious my relationship with "Patrick" was. That's what Pepper said I should call him to my family. But when we're alone, and he's fucking me with his hard candy dick, I call out Pepper every time, and he says, "fuck baby, milk my candy cock." It gets me off every time. Not to mention, he's the first person I had anal with, and that's saying something. It was a shock when he asked if he could put his candy cane there the first time, and I was in such an orgasmic haze I screamed yes.

Other than sex, we have a lot in common, but especially our love for the Christmas season. Though I'm always lonely on Christmas day, I love the holiday season—all holidays. But Christmas is my favorite. But when he asked if I was going to take him with me to my family's ranch, I knew I couldn't, but at the same time, I couldn't leave him alone. I want to spend as much time as possible with him.

I watch his favorite movie, Die Hard, on the TV when he jumps over my couch and settles beside me. He gets chocolate all over my sofa, but when he moves, it vanishes. The room is not too warm since I don't want him to melt, though he says he can't.

"So," he grabs some popcorn from the bowl I have in my lap. "You aren't a Bruce Willis fan?"

"I am," I clarify. "I'm just not super into action films."

"You like Home Alone," he teases.

"That's a family film, not an action movie like this."

"Half the film is a kid setting up increasingly lethal booby traps for the two most determined burglars in history." He chews on his popcorn, and I wonder where it goes. Does he even have a digestive system? How can a candy bar eat? Really, how is a candy bar alive? I guess I'm so desperate and lonely that I just accepted his Candyman self so quickly when he introduced himself. Then, I was even more desperate when he kissed me, and now, I can't get enough of him.

"It's a family film," I repeat.

"Right, right. You're so into family films, and yet you have a fascinating browsing history of porn on your computer."

"How did you—You looked through my computer?"

"You really should look that shit up on a private window. What you're into... We need to try some of that stuff." He winks at me.

"Oh my god. Stop! I'm not going to do... that stuff with you." I laugh.

"We already did some of it." He shrugs and smiles.

His white chocolate teeth are perfectly carved straight, except for one crooked incisor.

"So, tell me, *Liberty*," he likes to call me by my full name sometimes, which makes my heart skip a beat. No one calls me that. "How long are you going to keep me waiting?"

"Waiting for what?" I have a feeling I know what's coming. I haven't said the words to anyone in years, and the fear of telling a candy bar that I love him makes me feel like a loser. I'm in love with Pepper. I am, but he's not my future. Sometimes, I wonder if this is all just a dream. But in the morning, I wake up, go to my kitchen counter, and find Pepper sleeping. He peeks one eye open, winks at me, and then goes back to sleep.

I don't know if he sleeps until I get home or what he does during the day, but I know I can't be with a candy bar for life or someone who does nothing all day. Work ethic is vital to me, and being with someone who cares about that is important. But Pepper is in his box all day—What am I even thinking! He's a candy bar. It's not like he's able to have a job.

"Tell me how you feel about me, Libby. I want to know." He looks me straight in the eye, and my heart aches at thinking what I want to tell him but can't.

"I... Um..." I look down at the popcorn. He uses his hand to move and curls his candy cane fingers around my chin to pull my gaze to his. I feel my face grow sticky from the sugar and chocolate.

In a flash, it's like I'm looking at someone completely different. It's like his whole body flashes into a human form. He has soft brown eyes, bronze skin, and a naked torso packed with muscles. His hair is dark black, and he has an undercut haircut.

I'm about to say something when my eyes refocus, and he's just my Candyman boyfriend again. I shake my head. "I care for you, Pepper."

"Patrick, call me Patrick right now." His voice is rough. It's almost like the brown in his eyes becomes dark chocolate.

"Why Patrick?"

He shrugs and gives me a cocky grin. "I just want to feel human for a second."

"But you're not human."

His expression falls, but then it grows stern. "Is that why you won't say it? Tell me the truth. Tell me your real feelings, Liberty. Or you can't, can you? Because I'm not a real boy? Is that what's holding you back?"

"You're real!" I argue. "It's just..." I sigh and look at my hands. His hand on my chin drops, and tears well in my eyes. "I want a family."

"We can have a family. We can have little chocolate mints running around this living room." He sounds so serious, and it makes me angry.

"Pepper—"

"Patrick."

"Whatever! I want a house with a manicured lawn and flowers running up the walkway. I want a *human* husband who has a job but respects that I want to work too. I want to have children and grow old with someone and have normal human sex sometimes." That last part isn't entirely true anymore. "I want to have a big wedding with my whole family there and have kids that look like the perfect mix of my husband and me. I want to go to PTA meetings and come home and complain about it to my husband. You can't give me all of that, Pepper."

I look up at him. He's not looking at me. He gets up from the couch and starts pacing. "You don't know that. We've been together for almost a month now. We've gotten to know each other emotionally and sexually. I feel like you're the one for me, the one I've been waiting for my whole life for you. And if me being a chocolate bar is the only thing—"

"Pepper, you've been alive since what? When I bought you?"

"No," He snaps, then covers his mouth, his eyes growing wide.

"What...What does that mean?" My heartbeat speeds up, and a dash of hope enters my mind.

"I..." He nibbles on his lip. "I can't say."

"Tell me right now what's going on!"

"I can't," he sounds like he's desperate too. But he won't, and I don't know why. My mind wanders to the witch that created him. "Is it Mrs. Owens? Did she put a curse on you or something?" My eyes widen, and I think of all he's told me, about the family he dreamed he had if he grew up human, how he knows all this Christmas and movie trivia. I thought the fact that he was brought to life by my buying him meant that he was new to this world and liked everything I did because of some witchcraft... But maybe he wasn't created in a bakery... He likes Die Hard, and I never considered it a Christmas movie. What if...

My friend Katie had a bad breakup with her ice cream man. She didn't tell me much or anything. But she was depressed for a week before she met her human boyfriend. Alex looks very much like her ice cream lover, and she suspected that maybe her ice cream man was made with Alex's appearance in mind. But that never made sense to me.

Realization dawns on me. "She cursed you, didn't she? She made a human into a candy bar!"

He doesn't respond, and that's all the confirmation I need.

"That's horrible!"

He still says nothing.

"And let me guess, you can't talk about it."

He nibbles on his peppermint lips.

"Is the curse even breakable?"

He doesn't look me in the eye, and I'm getting fired up.

"What a wicked fucking witch!" I jump up and say, "Get in your box."

"Libby," he warns.

"Get in your box now, *Patrick*! I'm going to get you to be a human again." No wonder he wanted me to call him that. It's his name!

"Is that what you want? Just me as a human?"

My eyes widen.

"What about our time together? Don't you like my chocolate center?"

"I..."

"Is me being human all that matters to you?"

"No—"

"I don't believe you." He shakes his head. "I thought what we had was special. That you wanted me for me." His voice cracks.

I feel my heart breaking as I continue to tell him, "I do—"

"But you only want a human, don't you?" he spits. "I'm a candy bar. What can I offer you? I don't have a job, right?"

"That's not it."

"Are you a gold digger? Do you want a guy with a job so he can support you?"

"I said I wanted to work too!"

"And you want normal human kids, too." He scoffs. "Just the perfect little family."

"That's not it!"

"Are you prejudiced against chocolate, *Libby*? I thought you were better than that."

I want to scream at his use of my nickname. I'm Liberty to him. Not Libby.

"I am! I just..." Tears rain down my face.

My peppermint Candyman mutters, "Shit, I'm sorry. I don't know what I was thinking."

"I love you, Pepper! But I want a life more than just with chocolate. I have dreams of a family. They're dreams I've had for years. I want you! I would love chocolate babies with you, but what would people say? What would my family say?" I shut my eyes and think of a life with Pepper. It would be a life where he, a once-human chocolate bar, would give me the happiest years of my life. I'd get to eat his candy all the time. But could we have a family? Creating a chocolate baby in my belly is unheard of. Crazy even! But the thought of how we would be happy, how I'd come home to my chocolate husband holding our little candy baby that I'd kiss and rock to sleep, would be lovely. I'd have the best sex of my life, too, though it would be weird. I could tell my family about it, and they'd probably be freaked, but who cares? Mom would probably faint, but they'd be happy for me, right? Then we could grow old together, and I'd have my chocolate bar by my side with our little chocolate children standing around my bedside with their children, all being able to live forever and remember me by... Wait, would he ever expire?

I realize then that I don't care that he's chocolate. I don't know what people think. He could expire any day now, and if I don't tell him how I feel if I don't spend as much time with him as possible, I may never love again.

"I love you," I open my eyes. "You know what, I don't care what they think. As long as you don't have an expiration date, I want you by my side forever!"

I look up at Pepper to find not a man made of candy but a human. He has dark skin, deep brown eyes, and a soft smile. He's completely naked with the hottest body I've ever seen and dear god, his cock is glorious.

I gape at him. "P-Pepper?"

"Patrick." He says softly. His eyes gaze at me, and they're light and happy. "I love you too, Liberty. I'm so happy you've realized just how much you love me for me."

"I... You're human again. How is that possible?"

"You broke the spell. You admitted you loved me no matter what. This thing the witch does is to make sure that the person loves their lover despite their differences. And you do."

"I do." My heart is so full of love for this man.

I don't waste another second as I tackle him. He gasps as our mouths collide. He doesn't taste completely sweet anymore, but semi-sweet, like he's just eaten peppermint chocolate. We're making out, and he's pulling at my clothes when I feel wrong about something. I pull away from him just as he pulls my top off, revealing my breasts.

"God, you're beautiful. Merry Christmas, Liberty."

He goes to take my nipple into his mouth when I say, "Wait. I, uh... You'll never be chocolate again, will you?"

Realization dawns on him, and embarrassment consumes me, but he smirks. "You like chocolate sex too much, don't you, baby."

I bite my lip and nod.

"Well, don't worry," he shifts in front of me and becomes a candy bar again. "I can shift forms now and forever. We can have our human babies, and we can have the life you want, and we can also have some chocolate fun time, too."

"You promise?"

"Yes, and just to clarify, I do have a job. That's where I go when you go to work. I'm a hotel tycoon."

"And you became a chocolate?"

"I wanted someone to love me for me, Liberty, and that was you. I fell in love with you right away. We're so much alike, and I love you more than anything."

I smile so brightly and then kiss my candy man hard. I pull him down on top of me, and he presses his lips to mine. We kiss for a while, his chocolate melting onto my hot body. He leaves chocolate fingerprints on my arms as he holds them down and grinds his candy stick dicks hard against me. I moan as he presses between my legs. One dick toys with my clit while the other teases my entrance. I'm glad I wore a skirt today so he can fit in. And I didn't even wear panties.

With his strong fingers, he rips my skirt in half and hisses. "Fuck you're bare and beautiful. You've been a good girl this year."

"I think I'm being very bad with my candy bar." My peeked nipples are ready and waiting for the twisting abuse they get from his semicircle fingertips.

He moves his hands to my chest and takes a nipple between his candy cane fingers, and it curls, molding around my tip and then tugging. I cry out. Then he takes the other nipple in his mouth, and his chocolate tongue laps around me. It's always weird how his tongue feels so normal but tastes like chocolate.

"Are you ready for me, baby," he says against my tits.

"Mm," I look into his eyes and swear I see him in human.

"I just want to feel you with my regular dick just once before I fuck you hard with my candies."

"Promise to give me the hard stuff?"

"I promise, my good little Christmas slut." He growls and then shoves his thick long human cock into my pussy. He fills me up just as much as his candy cane does, only it's different in the sense that as he begins to slowly fuck me, I know this is lovemaking. He's making love to me as a human, and I like it. But right now, I need more of him.

I press my lips against his and growl, "I love a good orgasm, but I'd prefer a foodgasm."

He stills and then laughs and shifts into his candy bar self. His laughter dies, and his eyes turn dangerous with need. "I hoped you'd say that."

Then I feel his dick shift inside of me, and his other grow against my ass. I'm not prepared, but my juices from my pussy and his chocolate precum mix, and I know what he's about to do. He's no longer human, and he's all candy now. The harshness of his cane makes me moan as he thrusts into both my holes, and I cry out. I feel it expands as though he's growing and getting harder. His rounded tip hits me over and over again right where I need him most, and I start to convulse around him.

"That's right, milk my chocolate. Fuck you're such a good girl. I want to fill you with my minty seed."

"Minty...seed?" I say through my foodgasmic haze.

"You want a family. I've always wanted a family. I will support and love you until the end of time, Liberty. And that includes," He thrusts one more time and moans. He pulls out, and I watch as his chocolate and peppermint cum shifts turns to salty semen and sprays all over my chest. He catches his breath as he continues, "Filling you up with as much of my cum as possible to make you a mother."

"I'm going to get a UTI from having chocolate shoot up my vagina," I pant.

He laughs. "Believe me when I say, even though it always feels and looks like chocolate, it's the real deal, baby. Next time, with your consent, I want to try for a little chocolate mint."

My eyes well with tears.

"Is that a no? Did I scare you off? Our kids won't be food. I already asked Mrs. Owens about that stuff. I don't sign contracts without knowing what I'm getting into."

"I want kids with you. I want that family with you. I don't care if they're chocolate or human or what. I want you forever, Patrick."

"Good," he says, shifting back to his human self and collapsing beside me. He pulls me close to cuddle into his warm human frame.

I gaze upon the man candy I love as he says, "You know, it's Christmas Day Now."

I look over at my alarm clock and smile. "So it is."

"Merry Christmas, Liberty. I can't wait to spend the rest of my life with you."

I laugh. "Are you proposing to me?"

"Yes. I am." He shifts back into his chocolate self. It's so easy for him that I wonder what that's like. Then, he breaks off a piece of his chocolate and morphs it into a candy cane ring. It hardens, and he places it on my finger. It fits perfectly. "I'll get you a real one tomorrow. I promise."

"This is perfect." Tears fill my eyes. "Thank you."

"No." he kisses the top of my head. "Thank you for making me that happiest candy bar in the world."

He presses his lips to mine.

I pull away. "Merry Christmas, Patrick."

"Call me Pepper," He smirks.

"Pepper."

epilogue

. . .

ten years later

I love Christmas. It's the time of year that brought my husband and I together; our daughter Candace was born the year after. Then, two years later, Parker was born around New Year's, and three years ago, Penelope came along. This pregnancy, though, isn't a very Christmassy one.

Every child I've had either was born at Christmas or around it. But this baby is a Valentine's child. And I'm pretty sure that'll piss off my best friend Katie's sister since she's claimed Valentine's Day as hers forever. But our little Violet will be a Valentine's baby no matter what, according to Patrick.

I sit on our living room couch as the kids open their presents. Patrick walks over to me with a mug of hot cocoa, and I take it from him. "Thank you." I sip it and moan. "It's peppermint chocolate."

"Don't moan like that in front of the kids," he growls in my ears. "Or Christmas is going to end early for them."

"Mom, Dad! Stop being gross!" Candace says. She's got my sass but spends so much time with her Uncle Jason and his family that this girl has never gone a day without being sassy. Even as a toddler, she'd flip her hair and roll her eyes at me. Her first word was "no."

"No kissy, Daddy," Penelope says.

She jumps in between us and plops onto my lap. She hugs me close and glares at her father. She's a mama's girl, different from Candace, who is a daddy's girl all the way. Meanwhile, Parker seems to love us equally. And he manipulates us skillfully. He's a sneaky little boy who always asks why our house smells like peppermint or why mom has chocolate on her arm that vaguely resembles a hand's shape.

We vowed we'd never tell our kids our secret. Well, Patrick's secret. While Katie and Jason had decided to try the whole process of becoming edible monsters, I decided to stay human all these years.

After the kids went to bed, Patrick and I walked into the master, and I shut the door with my foot before prowling toward him. I push him onto the bed only for him to shift into his peppermint candy form, and his clothes disappear when he shifts. They end up on the floor beside the bed, and I want to laugh.

"You look so hot tonight, baby." He says

"I'm extremely pregnant, Patrick. I feel like a blimp."

"Is there anything I can do to make you feel better?"

I nibble on my lip. "I don't want you to freak out."

"I don't like the tone of this conversation."

"I, uh, well. I guess I'll show you."

I turn away from him and close my eyes before muttering the enchantment Mrs. Owens gave me and feeling my body morph into none other than a chocolate marshmallow candy bar.

I turn, and I find his jaw agape and his eyes wide. "You... But... I thought you didn't want to be candy. I thought it could be dangerous with the baby. Katie—"

"I talked to Mrs. Owens. If I do this once while pregnant, it shouldn't hurt our little Violet. But just... You'll have to wait for your marshmallow kisses until after she's born."

"Fuck you look good enough to eat." He licks his peppermint lips.

"Feel free to take a bite out of me." I try to sound sexy, but I feel so silly saying it.

He bursts out laughing, and so do I. Then he pulls me to him and kisses my squishy lips.

"I love you, Marshmallow girl. Merry Christmas."

"Merry Christmas."

Then he gives me the best peppermint kiss of my life.

note from the author

Here's a little extra something for you readers.

something extra

· · ·

pepper

*T*he moment I see Libby that's it for me. I'm hooked. I need this woman in my life, and seeing her pick me out in the store was the best thing that ever happened to me.

I'm pretty sure I hate my life except for maybe this moment. I've never been with someone who's with me for me, instead of with me for my money. I inherited my money from my family, and ever since women throw themselves at me for nothing more than wanting to be my pampered spoiled wife. No one wanted to get to know me. When women found out that I love Christmas they thought I was joking. They expected me to take them to dinner at a fancy restaurant and then fuck them in my hotel penthouse.

They didn't expect me to make a big deal about

tree lightings, or going to Candy Cane lane, something my mother would take me to when I was a child. I loved Candy Cane lane, so when Mrs. Owens asked me what kind of baked good I wanted to be, I said, "something with Candy Canes."

When Libby entered the store I swear it was love at first sight, and I knew that she would be the one for me. Then when I found out she loved Christmas, I knew we were meant to be.

That first night, she wasn't even surprised to find out that I was real. She was excited to fuck my candy cane dicks. She wanted nothing more than to have me take her in both holes, and then to suck on my minty balls before going between each cane with her tongue.

The last month has been nothing but heaven with her, and I want to spend the rest of my life with this woman, but I know that she has her issues with the fact of what I am. I want to tell her I'm human, but at the same time, I want her to fall in love with the real me before I tell her. Her finding out who I really am could ruin everything, but a slight bit of hope makes me want to reveal it all to her. Only, I need her to say the three words that will break the spell and make me hers forever.

As she sleeps the night before Christmas Eve I whisper in her ear, "I love you, Liberty."

She mumbles something in her sleep but I can't make it out, and because of that I know I can't turn into a person. Part of me never wants to turn into a person again. Sure, I turn into a human during the day, but I hate it, and waste the day when I'm in meetings or looking at fucking engagement rings for Libby, just wishing that she gets off of work and I can transport back to my candy box and become the man she wants nothing more than to fuck and eat.

But I don't want to wait any longer. It's now or never and tonight I'm determined to break the spell and find out how she truly feels. Because if Libby doesn't want me it will break my heart into a million shattered candy pieces. But if she does, I'll spend the rest of my life sweetening up her life and making her happy.

acknowledgments

There are a few people to thank for this story, but I especially want to thank Reina Diaz, the woman who inspired this story by calling a dick a popsicle. You are a fantastic artist and I'm so happy we met! I'm also so thankful for your artwork on this project and all the other projects! I'm so excited to work with you in the future.

I want to thank my bestie Nicole, who has been a great support as a fellow mom and book friend. You supported this project and told me to go for it. You are a great friend, and I am so thankful I have you in my life.

I also want to thank Booked Forever Shop for making this wonderful new cover for these stories! It's been a blast working with you!

I want to thank my husband, Jacob, who brainstormed ice cream-related jokes with me the day I decided to write this story. You are the love of my life, and I'm so happy we have each other. You make me laugh and are so encouraging that I don't know what I'd do without you.

about the author

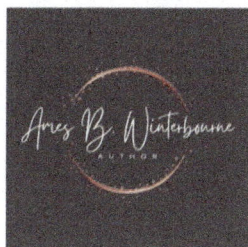

Ames is a mom, paralegal, and writer. She writes various genres of stories with spice, but *The Matchmaker Baker Series* is her first Monster Romance series.

When not writing, you can find gasping for breath as she chases after her little Loki toddler, cuddling with her cats, watching the Golden Girls with her husband, or reading a good most likely spicy book.

Sign up for my newsletter for more news, NSFW images, and fun surprises! Click here to subscribe!

facebook.com/amestheauthor

instagram.com/ames_the_author

tiktok.com/@amesbwinterbourne

goodreads.com/amesbwinterbourne

pinterest.com/amestheauthor

amazon.com/Ames-B-Winterbourne